SAINT BRIGID'S
BONES

SAINT BRIGID'S
BONES

A Celtic Adventure

PHILIP FREEMAN

PEGASUS BOOKS
NEW YORK LONDON

SAINT BRIGID'S BONES

Pegasus Books LLC
80 Broad Street, 5th Floor
New York, NY 10004

Copyright © 2014 Philip Freeman

First Pegasus Books edition October 2014

Interior design by Maria Fernandez

Ireland map courtesy of the author.

Library of Congress Cataloging-in-Publication Data is available.

ISBN: 978-1-60598-632-6

10 9 8 7 6 5 4 3 2 1

Printed in the United States of America
Distributed by W. W. Norton & Company

For Alison

THE
WESTERN
SEA

ULSTER

Armagh

Achill
Island

CONNACHT

Boyne R.

Tara

Lambay
Island

Liffey R.

Kildare

LEINSTER

THE
EASTERN
SEA

Aran
Islands

Sleaty

Glendalough

Cashel

Barrow
R.

Emly

MUNSTER

Skellig
Michael

IRELAND

SAINT BRIGID'S
BONES

Chapter One

I never meant to burn down the church.

That's what I kept telling myself as I stood in front of Sister Anna's hut.

It was a cool morning for mid October and dark clouds from the west threatened rain at any moment. Sister Anna was the abbess of the monastery of holy Brigid at Kildare. Her hut was a small structure made of rough-hewn grey stone with a thatch roof. When Brigid was alive she had cultivated a patch of bluebells and golden buttercups in front that made the place seem quite cheerful. But now the flowers were gone and nothing but a cold stone bench stood beside the wooden door.

I took a deep breath and knocked. I prayed that God would have mercy on my soul, for I knew Sister Anna would not.

"Come in."

I pushed open the door and stooped to enter the hut, careful to close the door gently behind me. Sister Anna sat at her desk beneath the single window in back writing on a piece of parchment. She did not look up.

The abbess was a woman of about sixty with white hair and dark eyes. She wasn't wearing her veil on her head at the moment, but this wasn't unusual as we seldom did so unless we were at worship. Like all the sisters, her tunic was of undyed wool spun and woven into a simple cloth and tied around the waist with a leather belt. We looked quite similar to women of the druidic order except that their clothing was bleached white and each wore a small golden torque around her neck. Instead of a torque, we wore a plain wooden cross.

Sister Anna wrote with her left hand, which was understandable as her right arm hung uselessly at her side. The right side of her face was also deeply scarred, obviously from some accident years ago, but she never spoke of it and no one dared to ask. To say she was stern would have been an understatement, but I had a great deal of respect for her, as did the other sisters. I don't believe I had ever seen her smile. She was a devout Christian woman and an able leader. Her style was different from that of Brigid, but in the decade since our founder had died she had held the monastery together and continued our mission against formidable odds.

"Sister Deirdre, come and stand before my desk where I can see you better."

Even after her many years in Ireland, I could always hear a faint British accent in her voice. I moved into the hut and stood where she told me.

"Brother Fiach has told me what happened at the church at Sleaty, but I want to hear what you have to say. Tell me, but keep it brief, if that is possible for you."

I cleared my throat and began.

"As you know, I left our monastery a few days ago with two of the sisters to finish preparations for the new church at Sleaty across the Barrow River. We arrived just as the tenant farmers from the monastery, who had been helping with the construction, were leaving to return here for the harvest. Brother Fiach had stayed to finish carving the stone cross in front of the church. He had used some of the stones from the old Roman trading post there. Of course, the last of the Roman merchants left years ago after—"

"I said brief, Sister Deirdre. I don't need a history lesson."

"Yes, I'm sorry. Well, Brother Fiach was putting the final touches on the cross when we arrived. He had finished the wooden altar the previous day as well as the beds in the back room for the sisters who would be staying there through the winter. I was impressed that everything had been made from solid oak, like our church here. The Sleaty church could hold at least thirty worshippers standing close together. Father Ailbe once told me that in one of the churches he visited in Rome, the wealthy parishioners actually sat on wooden pews, though I really can't imagine why they—"

"Sister Deirdre!"

"Yes, brief, I'm sorry, Sister Anna. Well, I couldn't sleep that night, even though I was exhausted, so after the others went to bed I went into the church and lit a candle on the altar. I knew that we didn't have many candles left and it was a terrible waste, not to mention dangerous with all the sawdust still around, but I needed to pray and the light in the darkness helped. While I knelt there, I admired the linen cloth on the altar that had been embroidered by Brigid herself. It was bordered with intricate, interlaced patterns in green and gold along the edges, with fantastic, richly colored animals and angels dancing in the center. I thought it was a beautiful adornment for the new church. I was also thinking how proud Brigid would have been of the work we had done."

I paused for a moment, thinking of how much I had loved looking at that cloth in our church at Kildare since I was a little girl. I knew many had attributed healing powers to it.

"Continue, Sister Deirdre."

"Well, I prayed at the altar for a long time. I thought I heard something at one point and went outside to check, but there was no one there, so I went back inside. It must have been the flickering shadows on the walls that finally lulled me to sleep. The next thing I knew Brother Fiach was dragging me out the church door. I was coughing and choking and could barely see anything with all the smoke around me. I suddenly remembered the altar cloth of Brigid and started back into the church to get it, but Fiach pulled me away. I kicked him and screamed that I had to find the cloth, but thankfully he didn't let go. I would have died if he hadn't held me back. The two sisters were running with buckets to bring water from the well, even though it was clearly hopeless. The fire was devouring the freshly-cut oak and had turned the church into a raging inferno. There was nothing the four of us could do but fall on our knees as we watched the church burn. We huddled together all night beside the stone cross, warming ourselves on the embers of the dying fire with a single blanket wrapped around us. By morning there were only smoking ruins."

For a long time Sister Anna simply looked at me without saying a word. I swallowed hard and braced myself for the storm I knew was coming. Then at last she spoke.

"Needless to say, I am most disappointed."

"I'm so sorry, Sister Anna, I didn't mean to—"

"Sister Deirdre, for once be quiet and listen to me."

I nodded with my head bowed and allowed her to continue.

"I have sent a message to King Bran, who owns the lands at Sleaty, to let him know what happened and to ask that we might be allowed to begin again in the spring. I hold out little hope that he will grant this request. The agreement to lease his land specified that the church must be completed by the end of October. Bran is not a forgiving man, therefore we must consider the project at Sleaty effectively dead. There will be no mission in Munster and no support for the monastery from that source."

I continued to stand silently.

"You're an intelligent woman, so I won't explain to you what that loss means for us. Do you see this abacus on my desk?"

I nodded that I did.

"Let me just say that I have been calculating how long we can continue operating with our current supplies and projected harvest. If my figures are correct, we'll begin running low on food this coming spring and will have to start turning the needy away, the first time we have done so in the fifty years since Brigid founded this monastery. Perhaps the donations from pilgrims at holy Brigid's day in February will be large enough to see us through the summer, though I doubt it. I was counting on the harvest from the new church at Sleaty to supplement our stores beginning next autumn. Now there will be nothing."

She stood up and walked from behind her desk to stand in front of me. She was a small woman, but her presence more than made up for her stature.

"Brother Fiach has taken full responsibility for what happened at Sleaty."

I started to protest but she raised her hand.

"No, don't speak. I'm not interested in assigning blame. I know how the fire began, but it's too late to change that now. I am not going to punish you."

I must have looked shocked.

"Oh, I know you'd like me to put you on bread and water until Easter or some such penance, but frankly, Sister Deirdre, I fail to see what good that would do. Instead, let me ask you a question and I expect an honest answer: Are you happy here at the monastery?"

I had never heard the abbess ask anyone if they were happy before.

"Yes, Sister Anna. I've spent most of my life here, when I wasn't with my grandmother just down the road. I grew up with Brigid and the sisters and Father Ailbe. I know I only took vows three years ago, but this place is my home."

"Somehow, I don't think you're being honest with me—or yourself. You grew up here, indeed, but you grew up in another world of druids and bards as well. I don't doubt that you are trying to be a good Christian, but I'm not convinced you want to be a nun. I can't help wondering if you came to us at a time of tragedy in your life because we were convenient."

There was too much truth in what she said for me to deny it outright, but it was more complicated than she made it seem. At least I hoped so.

"It's true, Sister Anna, that part of the reason I joined the monastery is because I've always been comfortable here. But my desire to be a sister of Brigid's order and to serve God is sincere. I know I'm not like the rest of the sisters. I come from the Irish nobility. I was trained as a professional bard. My father was a great warrior, though a pagan. My grandmother is a druid seer. But my mother was a baptized Christian, as am I. Though, if I may ask, what does this have to do with the fire at Sleaty?"

"Nothing, perhaps. I'm not accusing you of burning down the church because you're unhappy here. I'm simply wondering if the reason such a thing could happen is because you don't have your mind on your work. Don't forget, Sister Deirdre, I've known you since you were a little girl. You were always a joyful person with great focus on what you wanted to achieve in life. You're the best student our school ever produced and, I know, one of the finest bards in Ireland. But since you took your vows I've seen little joy or purpose in you. I know what you lost. I am sympathetic. But you are like a ship adrift in a storm and I can no longer wait for you to find safe harbor."

Sister Anna walked over to gaze out the window, then turned back to me.

"I'm not ordering you to leave these walls. But as your abbess, I am requiring that you prayerfully consider what it is you are searching for here. This place is a refuge of sorts for all of us—there's no shame in that. It will be a haven for those in need as long as it exists, which may not be much longer. But the primary mission of our order is to serve God by serving others. We are not a guest house for lost souls, Sister Deirdre. If your focus is not on our Lord and ministering to the needy of this land, then there is no place for you here."

I didn't know what to say. I simply stood there looking down at the dirt floor.

Suddenly, there was a shout outside the hut and Garwen burst through the door without even knocking.

"Sister Anna! They're gone! They're gone!"

Sister Anna had always insisted on protocol. For someone to rush into her hut uninvited was behavior that would have earned even a child a good lashing.

"Sister Garwen, what is the meaning of this? How dare you enter here without my leave. Get out this instant! I'll see you in the church later to discuss your punishment."

"But Sister Anna, I've just come from the church and they're gone! I was there to clean and polish them just like you told me to. I brought wine to wash them and a new woolen cloth to wrap them in, but they're gone!"

"What on earth are you talking about, child? What is gone?"

"The bones!" Garwen sank to her knees as she spoke. "The bones of holy Brigid—they're gone!"

7

Chapter Two

T
he first few hours after the discovery of the missing bones were chaotic. Everyone was in shock. Sister Anna immediately told Garwen to send the brothers to the gates of the monastery to stop anyone trying to leave. The abbess then rushed to the church with me two steps behind. I suppose I thought I could be of some help, but mostly I had to see the empty chest for myself.

Sister Anna pushed through the ill-fitting door on the sisters' side of the church and went to the altar in front. It was a simple wooden table with a golden crucifix on top. The silver paten for the Eucharist sat next to it, but both were untouched. On the right side of the altar was a stone slab marking the tomb beneath of Conláed, our first bishop, who had died many years before. On the left side was the small oaken chest holding Brigid's bones. There had never been a lock on it, only an iron latch tied with a crimson ribbon that once belonged to Brigid herself. The lid was wide open, as Garwen had left it. The small jug of wine for cleaning the bones, a few old rags, and the new woolen cloth all lay beside the chest where Garwen had dropped them before rushing out. The spilled wine had spread across the stone paving of the floor and was already soaking through the joints into the ground beneath it.

"Dear God in heaven," whispered Sister Anna as she peered into the blackness of the chest.

She knelt and touched the rough wooden bottom. The bones were always kept tightly bound in a leather sack, which was also missing. Sister Anna rested her head against the edge of the chest and closed her eyes, whether in prayer or anguish I couldn't tell. I knelt beside her and worked up the nerve to place my hand on her shoulder in comfort. I felt her stiffen at once. She rose quickly and stared at me with hard eyes. If she had seemed on the verge of tears a moment ago, it had quickly passed.

"Sister Deirdre," she said sharply, "go and bring Sister Garwen back immediately."

I ran out of the church and found Garwen weeping on the bench in front of our scriptorium. She was in such distress that I practically had to carry her back to Sister Anna.

"Sister Garwen," abbess said when we had returned, "did you touch anything after opening the chest? Anything at all?"

"No—no—Sister Anna—I swear—nothing," Garwen managed between sobs. I thought she was about to collapse.

Sister Anna grabbed her by the shoulders and shook her.

"Look at me, you fool of a girl. There isn't time for this now! Was there any sign that someone had been in the chest before you? Was the ribbon untied? Was the latch open? Did you see anyone leaving the church?"

"No, no—Sister Anna—I—didn't see or hear—anyone. The church was—empty when I arrived. The latch—was closed and tied—just like it—always is."

Sister Anna turned away and swore under her breath, something I had never heard her do before.

"Garwen," I said, as I took her hand and held it gently. "Please, try to remember something for me. Was there any dust on the latch when you opened it?"

The question surprised her and she seemed to calm down as she considered it. Sister Anna turned back suddenly and looked first at me, then Garwen.

"Dust? Well, yes, Deirdre, there was."

"Are you sure? Absolutely sure?" the abbess asked.

"Yes, Sister Anna, I'm positive. I remember kneeling in front of the chest to untie the ribbon and noticing how much dust had collected on the latch. I was embarrassed that it was so dirty. I untied the ribbon, then dipped one of the rags in the wine and wiped the latch clean before opening the chest."

"*Mudebroth!*" said Sister Anna, which I took to be a British curse word. I didn't ask her what it meant.

"Sister Garwen, go and tell the sisters to search all the buildings. Look everywhere. Send someone back here immediately if you find anything unusual, anything at all."

"Yes, Sister Anna." Garwen bowed and left the church.

The abbess and I were alone in the church once again.

"Sister Deirdre, you realize of course this makes matters much worse. If there was dust on the latch, it could have been weeks since the chest was opened and the bones stolen. The last time the bones were cleaned was early August. They could be anywhere on the island by now."

"Yes, Sister Anna."

The abbess began to search around the altar. I knelt by the chest again and looked inside. It was as empty as a tomb.

"Close the chest, Sister Deirdre. It will be too painful for everyone to see it empty."

"Yes, Sister Anna."

I pulled the heavy lid over on its hinges and brought it down gently. It made a lonely, hollow sound as I shut it and fixed the latch. I started to tie the ribbon when I noticed something strange.

"Sister Anna, look at this. It's different!"

The abbess knelt by the front of the chest and looked at the latch.

"It seems the same latch to me, Sister Deirdre. What are you talking about?"

"No, Sister Anna, not the latch, the ribbon. We've always used Brigid's ribbon of fine red linen to tie the latch shut. But feel this."

She took the ribbon from my hands and ran her fingers along it.

"Sister Anna, it looks exactly like the ribbon we've always used. Even by touch most people couldn't tell the difference, but this isn't linen, it's—"

"Byzantine silk," she said. "My mother had a ribbon made from it. I still remember the smoothness of the weave. It was her greatest treasure."

"Yes, Sister Anna."

"But why, Sister Deirdre, would someone replace the linen ribbon with a piece of silk?"

"They must have wanted the original ribbon as well as the bones—perhaps for the healing properties her possessions are thought to possess."

Sister Anna considered my words for a moment.

"Yes, I suppose it would make sense to take the ribbon. It belonged to Brigid and was close to her bones every day for ten years."

"Sister Anna," I said hesitantly, "I think this tells us something about the thief. Maybe more than one thing."

"Go on, Sister Deirdre."

"Silk ribbons are a luxury item. They come only on the few ships that make their way from Constantinople to Gaul and then on to Britain and Ireland. This one ribbon would cost more than any Irish farmer could afford."

"Yes," she said, "my father saved everything he could for months to buy one for my mother, and that was in Britain where such things are more common."

"Exactly. The only people in Ireland who can afford such an item are the nobility—landowners, cattle lords, and kings. Whoever took the bones was wealthy."

I owned such a ribbon myself, though deep blue in color. It was given to me by a local lord for composing a song of praise. It was stored away now with my bardic robes in my grandmother's hut.

"What else do you think the ribbon tells us, Sister Deirdre?"

"That whoever took the bones had been here before. This ribbon was chosen ahead of time because it's almost identical to the one it replaced. The thief didn't want anyone to notice, at least not right away, that he had switched them."

"Yes, Sister Deirdre, that makes sense as well, but it doesn't narrow down the suspects in any helpful way. Hundreds of people come to this church every month to pray before Brigid's bones. Many of them placed their hands on this chest and saw her ribbon."

"Well, I suppose you're right."

She raised her eyebrows.

"I mean, of course you're right, Sister Anna."

Someone had stolen the bones of holy Brigid. I could hardly make myself believe it.

It wasn't a matter of who could have gotten into the chest— everyone had access to the church day and night—but who would dare to do such a terrible thing. To steal the bones of Brigid was an unthinkable blasphemy.

After the search of the monastery grounds yielded nothing, we spread out to the neighboring farms questioning everyone, even children. Had they seen anything suspicious? Had they heard anything about the bones?

I went to the landholdings southeast of the monastery on the broad grasslands stretching toward the Liffey River. Most people I talked to hadn't seen anything unusual. No one had heard a word about the bones. When I told them what had happened, they were in shock. Christian or not, they couldn't believe anyone would dare to disturb the bones of Brigid.

The last farm I came to that evening was on the border of the monastery lands and belonged to Tamun, a crusty old widower who raised apples and chickens. I knocked on his door and waited for an answer.

"You'll be standing there the whole damn night if you're waiting for me to come out."

Tamun was coming up the path from the stream with a bucket of water.

"Greetings to you, Tamun. I'm sorry to disturb you but I—"

"Yes, yes, the bones of Brigid were stolen and you're asking everyone if they saw anything. News travels fast around here."

He put the bucket down by the door but didn't invite me inside.

"Have you seen anything? You've always had a sharp eye, Tamun."

"Don't bother flattering me, Deirdre. I'm a mean old man, just like everyone says. It doesn't seem like that long ago since I set my dogs on you and your friends for trying to steal apples from my trees."

"I was six years old, Tamun."

"Humph. Well, I don't know who took the bones. Though there was something strange recently—a man hiding in the bushes by my stream a couple of weeks ago. It was a night when you nuns kept ringing that damn church bell."

"On Michaelmas?"

"Whatever. Anyway he was a tall fellow with a big sword. I chased him out from behind a hawthorn tree with my hoe and nearly caught him!"

"You chased an armed warrior with a hoe?"

"By the gods, yes! I don't let any damn stranger on my lands without asking, and even then I always say no. You should have seen him run! He flew out of there so fast a piece of his cloak was torn off on the thorns. I'll chase him out again if he ever comes back."

"Tamun, what did his cloak look like? What color was it? What pattern?"

He reached into his pocket and pulled out a rag.

"See for yourself. I've been using the piece that ripped off to blow my nose."

I took the small, damp rag and looked at it in the last of the fading light. It was a tartan weave of dark green-dyed wool with black and gold diagonals. Every tribe and clan had their own favorite pattern passed down through the generations. I didn't recognize this one, but it looked like a Leinster weave from our own province. It was a fine piece of work. Whatever wife had made this for her husband would be none too pleased that he had torn a hole in a cloak it had taken her months to make. Farmers wore tartans as well, but they were simple checked weaves made from coarse wool. This cloak had been made for a member of the warrior nobility.

"May I have this, Tamun?"

"Sure, keep the damn thing. I don't need it."

"Thank you. A good evening to you, Tamun."

"Just leave me in peace or I'll set the dogs on you again."

I walked back to the monastery through the darkness. A Byzantine ribbon and a warrior with a fine cloak hiding in the woods on the border of our church lands. I wondered if he could have taken the bones? Michaelmas was the feast of the angels celebrated at the end of September, plenty of time for dust to collect on the chest latch. But why would a nobleman want the bones of Brigid?

When three frantic, sleepless days of searching had passed, the sisters and brothers all gathered in the church to pray on our knees that our holy founder might speak to the misguided soul who had taken her remains and urge him to return them safely. Believers from the more distant farms and settlements arrived to ask if the news was true and joined us in supplication. We questioned them as well. Weeping and wailing could be heard throughout the monastery at all hours. It was as if someone had stolen a mother away from her children.

I gave Sister Anna the piece of the cloak from Tamun's farm. She didn't recognize the weave either, but placed it in a small wooden box along with the silk ribbon we had taken from the church. She was also surprised that a warrior would be hiding on the border of our lands. Still, as I thought about it, noblemen often passed through Kildare on their way to the west or south. It was a natural crossroads for this part of Ireland. Perhaps the stranger had simply been waiting for a friend by the stream and was spooked by a crazy old man with a hoe. Or maybe he was meeting a woman.

Sister Anna sent word to Father Ailbe urging him to return home as soon as possible. He had left for Munster after morning prayers two weeks earlier to visit friends. I was worried about him travelling that far alone since he was over eighty years old, but he insisted he could still take care of himself.

I walked with him westward from the monastery for over an hour just to make sure he would be alright. He wouldn't even let me carry his satchel. Then he smiled and said it was time for me to turn back. I kissed him on the cheek and watched as he moved at a slow but steady pace down the road. I was relieved when we later got word he had arrived safely.

A week after the bones were found missing, Sister Anna received a note from him saying that he had gotten her message and was returning to Kildare as quickly as his legs would carry him. He said the seriousness of the situation would have prompted him to ask the king at Cashel for the loan of a chariot and driver, but he was afraid his own bones wouldn't survive the trip.

Chapter Three

T hat night after evening prayers I walked through the empty monastery grounds. It was late, but I had a feeling most of the younger brothers and sisters would be gathered in the cooking hut. In happier times we would sit around the fire at night, drink beer, and sing, keeping it quiet so Sister Anna wouldn't hear. It was a great way to unwind after a long day's work.

"Deirdre, wait for me!"

It was Dari, running from the children's hut. I knew she must have just gotten them to sleep. We had been so busy the last few days that I had scarcely found any time to talk with her. She was my best friend at the monastery and the same age as me. Her real name was Darerca, but everyone except Sister Anna called her Dari. She was slightly shorter than me with light blond hair and pale blue eyes. Dari was the sort of person everyone instantly liked. She was unfailingly kind and thoughtful, full of common sense, and respectful of others' privacy. I, on the other hand, as Dari like to remind me, was impulsive, opinionated, and nosy.

"I feel like I haven't seen you in ages." She put her arm through mine and gave me a kiss. Leave it to Dari; even when everyone else in the monastery looked as if they were in mourning, she greeted me with a bright smile.

"I've been staying with the girls at night the last week since the children have been so upset. Some of the little ones are still crying themselves to sleep. None of them can focus on our lessons, not that I blame them. They're scared, Deirdre. So am I."

Dari was the teacher of the youngest children at the monastery. Parents from all over the island would send their sons and daughters to us for an education. We welcomed everyone, rich and poor, Christian or not. We even had a few children of druids among our students. Dari loved them all, perhaps all the more since she hadn't been able to have any of her own.

Dari and I had both been in unhappy marriages before we took our vows. She had been born near the sea in Ulster, the youngest of many children on a poor farm. Her father was a cruel man who didn't hesitate to beat his wife or children. When he bothered to speak to Dari at all, it was to yell at her to bring him more ale or berate her for being such a little fool. Her mother was a timid woman, too busy trying to avoid her husband's blows to care about her daughter. The only member of the family who showed her any love was an older brother who protected her as best he could from their father's anger, even though it earned him many a blackened eye. She was devastated when, in her tenth year, he was killed by outlaws who raided their farm.

Dari's father sold her in marriage to a local pig farmer when she was barely twelve. Her new husband drank even more heavily than her father and used her hard, beating her if she dared to cry. He was furious when she couldn't become pregnant and give him a son. Dari wouldn't tell even me some of the worst things he had done to her. One cold night, when she was seventeen, he fell drunk into their well and couldn't climb out. He called to her to throw him a rope or he would kill her, but she huddled in their hut with her hands over her ears and did nothing while he froze to death. Even though the brute deserved his fate, Dari was tormented with guilt for letting him die.

As a young widow, the law said she must return to her father's home so he could choose a new husband for her, but instead she ran away and met a kindly old priest named Ibar who told her of a God who loved those in need and forgave all sins. After some months of instruction, he veiled her as a nun. Her father was outraged when he found out, but the church had become her legal guardian and there was nothing he could do about it. Over the next few years, she gathered a small group of abandoned and abused women about her and formed a Christian community near Armagh, though the abbot there eventually drove them away. She then brought her little band south to Kildare and was welcomed into Brigid's monastery, just a year before I took my own vows.

"I'm scared too, Dari," I replied.

"Should we go in with the others or head back to our quarters?" she asked.

"We'd better go in. I haven't really talked to anyone for days and I want to find out how they're doing."

Dari nodded and opened the door to the cooking hut for me. Just as I suspected, there were a half-dozen men and women sitting around the fire. Most of them greeted us as we walked in, but not with the usual warmth and cheer. Sister Eithne glared at me. We had an unspoken pact of mutual loathing even in the best of times. She was a year older than me and we had gone to the monastery school together. On the first day of class she deliberately broke my new wax writing tablet. She and her little group of friends were always whispering about me behind my back. She hated that I would show her up in front of the nuns in spite of her best effort to be their favorite. Everyone thought we would grow out of our animosity as the years went by. We didn't.

I will grant that Eithne had a special gift for working with the poor widows who found a home at our monastery. She would spend hours every day talking to the lonely ones and tending to the sick and dying among them. Still, her kind heart didn't stop her from making my life as miserable as possible.

A couple of the other sisters moved over on a bench to make room for us. Brother Fiach, the carver, passed us a cup of milk. No one felt like drinking beer that night.

We talked for a few minutes about the weather, but I could tell no one had the heart for small talk. At last Fiach asked the question on everyone's mind.

"Deirdre, what do you think will happen if we can't find the bones?"

"I wish I knew. Brigid's bones drew pilgrims to our church along with their donations of food for our ministry. Our stores were already low. Without the bones and their healing power, I'm afraid visitors will stop coming altogether. I don't know if we'll be able to feed ourselves for long, not to mention the needy. And now that I've burned down the church at Sleaty, we won't be getting any food from there next fall."

Brother Kevin spoke up.

"Deirdre, you've got to quit blaming yourself for that. It could have happened to any of us."

"Yes, it could have," I said, "but I was the one who fell asleep with the candle burning."

Kevin shook his head. We had grown up together and he knew me too well to argue when I was indulging in self-pity. He wasn't a man of many words in any case, though he was kindhearted and always generous. He was tall and handsome with golden hair and muscles like a blacksmith underneath his robes. More than one impure thought had passed through my mind about him over the years, but I had to laugh at the idea. Kevin was the holiest person I'd ever known. He was always up before the rest of us praying in the church and was the last to leave each night. He fasted every Friday even though it wasn't required. He never so much as looked at a woman.

Suddenly Eithne spoke up.

"Quit blaming herself, Kevin? I blame her and I'm not the only one."

The bitterness in her voice was chilling.

"Deirdre, have you thought about what the fire you started means? It's the end of everything we've worked for here. It means starvation. Even while the bones were still in their chest we were hanging on by a thread. The church at Sleaty was our only hope for a steady supply of new food."

I saw Dari was about to say something, but I put my hand on her knee. Eithne was entitled to speak her mind. I deserved it.

"No food means no future," she continued. "It means the school will close down and the widows will be sent away. They have no families to care for them. Do you really think they'll find someone to take them in? Practically everyone on this island is hungry with the bad harvests of the last few years. The monks at Armagh will bar their gates and leave the starving in the cold to die. You can always go back to living with your grandmother and playing your little harp for kings and princes, but the widows have no place to go. A lot of us have no place to go."

She put her head in her hands and started to cry. Dari went to sit beside her and put her arm around her shoulders. I knew Eithne was the only child of poor parents from the Wicklow Mountains who had died recently. She had gone home just that summer to bury them. Their small, rocky farm had been seized by the nobleman who owned it and turned into a sheep pasture. Eithne was in her early thirties, old for a poor woman to find a husband. She had given up her youth and hopes for children to become a sister of holy Brigid.

Kevin spoke for a second time that night, a new record for him.

"Eithne, you know Deirdre didn't mean to burn down the church at Sleaty. If we can't forgive each other our sins and shortcomings, we don't deserve to call ourselves Christians."

Eithne wiped away her tears.

"You're right, Kevin." Then she turned to me. "But it's hard to forgive some people."

Fiach got up to pour everyone more milk from the pitcher before he spoke again.

"What happened at Sleaty is over," he said. "The fact remains that our monastery is in serious trouble now. What will we do if we can't find the bones? I don't see how Kildare will survive without them. Where will we go?"

We all sat in silence. It wasn't as if there were many options for nuns and monks in Ireland. We could try to form a new monastery somewhere, but few kings would welcome us onto lands they could make a better profit from with other tenants.

"We could try working something out with the monks at Armagh," suggested Sister Garwen, the nun who had discovered that the bones were missing. "Maybe they would be willing to accept us onto their lands to continue our work."

Dari shook her head.

"Garwen, you don't know the abbot like I do. I grew up in Ulster and tried to start a community there, but he wouldn't allow it. He can't stand the thought of women in positions of power. And he has close ties with all the Uí Néill kings north of the Liffey. He won't let us carry on our ministry there. He might take us into his monastery, but it would only be as his slaves."

The Uí Néill confederation of tribes, the sworn enemies of Leinster, home of our monastery, controlled the northern half of the island and were pushing ever southward against us. They were rich, powerful, and ruthless in their efforts to control all of Ireland. The abbot came from a prominent Uí Néill family and although he was supposedly neutral in secular affairs, he did everything he could to expand their rule at our expense.

"Maybe we could go west," said Fiach. "I've heard there are monks on Skellig Michael off the coast."

"Yes," I said. "There are a few monasteries on the mainland as well. I know Father Brendan started one recently. But those are small communities dedicated to contemplation and prayer, not service. The followers of Brigid are devoted to the poor and needy. We can't serve people if we live on deserted islands and empty coasts."

"What about Britain then? Father Ninian's old church in the land of the Picts has fallen on hard times lately and could use some help."

"Fiach, how could we leave Ireland?" I asked. "For most of us, this is home. This is where Brigid labored so long to build her monastery. To leave here would be to give up her dream as well as ours. And what about Father Ailbe? He's been on this island for decades and would never abandon it."

Father Ailbe had given his life to the Irish. We might leave, but he never would.

"The simple truth," I declared, "is that we have to find a way to continue our work at Kildare, bones or not. Our ministry is here, at this monastery, not in Britain or even somewhere else in Ireland. This is the center of everything Brigid built with her sweat and love. And remember, she didn't choose this place at random. Even the druids say there is something special about Kildare, as if Brigid knew that this was a place of unearthly power and possibility."

My listeners nodded. It was something we all felt, monks, nuns, and visitors alike, even those who put no stock in the old ways of magic and spirits.

"The soul of Brigid is here at Kildare, even if her bones are gone," I said. "This is where our work must live and prosper."

They seemed to have cheered up a little as we left the cooking hut and went to our sleeping quarters for the night, but Eithne still looked angry. The beds of all the nuns—except Sister Anna, who had her own quarters—were lined against each side of the hut with a simple wooden chest at the foot of each for the few personal possessions we each had. The hut was nothing but a large rectangular room about thirty feet long with no decoration except a cross on the wall above the door, but it was warm and dry with a peat fire always burning in the center. Dari and I had our beds next to each other nearest the door. The older nuns were closest to the fire, with Eithne's bed at the opposite side of the room as far from me as was possible. While she was washing at a basin in the back of the hut I screwed up my courage and went to stand beside her.

"Eithne, I wish we could put the past behind us and be friends."

She dried her face with a rag.

"I'm sorry to disappoint you, Deirdre, but I don't want to be your friend. You've brought nothing but pain to me since you were six years old. I hated that you were always smarter than me, even though I was the older one. I hated that the boys always thought you were so pretty. I hated that you came from a wealthy family. Then, just when I thought you were out of my life forever, you came back and joined the monastery as a nun. You, the least likely nun I've ever met. You could have married a king or a wealthy nobleman. Why did you have to come back here to torment me again? You, with all your talents, your gifts, your advantages. You have everything I ever wanted."

She threw the rag on table and practically hissed at me.

"I hated you when you were a girl, Deirdre, and I still do. If I could do something to drive you from this monastery, I would. But it doesn't look like I'll need to now that you've burned down the church at Sleaty and killed us all. Maybe whoever stole the bones did us a favor. Now we can just die and get it over with."

I stood there in shock, not knowing what to say.

"Go to bed, Deirdre, and leave me alone."

I crossed back to my side of the hut, shaking, took off my clothes, and crawled under my blankets. Dari was already asleep in the bed next to me. She looked as if she didn't have a care in the world.

I lay awake for a long time thinking about what Eithne had said. I couldn't believe the fury in her voice. I thought about when we were teenagers and she had been so fond of Cormac, a young prince from Glendalough who was also a student at our school. She did everything she could to get him to like her. I know a few times she snuck out of the girls' sleeping quarters and met him under the tree by the stream. I followed her once and saw them making love in the moonlight. She was on top of him and saw me spying on them from behind the bushes. I thought she would be embarrassed or angry, but she just smiled at me, as if in triumph.

A few weeks after that Cormac began to pay attention to me instead. My guess was he had grown tired of Eithne. A peasant girl wasn't the sort of woman a prince could marry anyway, as she must have known. One night I snuck out and met Cormac under that same tree. I had never been with a man before, but I think Cormac knew that. He was gentle and wonderful. When we finished, I lay happily in his arms with a blanket pulled over the two of us. Cormac was sleeping next to me when I heard a branch crack in the woods behind us. I looked up and saw Eithne staring at me with a look of such pain on her face that I wanted to go to her and tell her I was sorry. She left us there and we never spoke of it. Cormac and I spent many nights together under that tree over the next few years, then he went home to Glendalough to help his father rule his small kingdom. He and I saw each other from time to time and were always friends, but the passion we had known in school and the dreams I had of being with him faded away. Still, I often thought of him and our nights together, even after I became a nun.

Lying in my bed in the sisters' sleeping quarters that night with Eithne's angry words still echoing in my ears, I listened to the wind blowing through the trees outside. It sounded like a storm was coming. Finally I began to drift off to sleep.

But somewhere in the space between sleeping and waking, I heard a voice whispering to me:

Go back to the fire.

I sat up in bed and looked around. Everyone was asleep and all was quiet inside the hut. I threw on my cloak and rushed outside. There was no one there. I searched the ground for footprints near the wall closest to my bed, but there was nothing, even though the earth was damp from a light rain. Tired, wet, and feeling rather foolish, I went back to my bed and crawled under the covers. I heard Dari stir beside me.

"What were you doing outside, Deirdre?" she whispered.

"Nothing. I was just dreaming. Go back to sleep."

"What was the dream about?"

"Nothing, Dari, it was just a voice. An old woman whispering."

"What did she say?"

"She said for you to go to sleep."

"No, really."

"She said to go back to the fire, whatever that means."

"Hmm. Maybe she wants you to go to the cooking hut and bring us a midnight snack."

"It was just a silly dream. It doesn't mean anything. And I'm too tired to talk about it. Good night, Dari."

"Good night, Deirdre. Sweet dreams."

Chapter Four

E arly the next morning, Sister Anna called me to her hut once more. I stood outside the door, wondering if somehow she was going to blame me for the missing bones, then I knocked.

"Come in."

Our abbess looked as if she hadn't slept for days, which was probably the case. I stood in front of her desk once more as she read by the faint light of a single oil lamp with the wick trimmed well back.

"Frugality, Sister Deirdre," she said as she saw me looking at the lamp. "I've always practiced it, though now it is needed more than ever."

She put down the letter she had been reading.

"I'm afraid, Sister Deirdre, that circumstances don't permit me to continue our previous discussion about your troubled spirit this morning. Other, more pressing matters demand our attention. To be blunt, we face the greatest threat in the history of our monastery. A few days ago I told you that our community faced a crisis. Now we face a catastrophe. Without the bones of holy Brigid, pilgrims will cease to come to Kildare. The food and offerings those visitors bring are essential to the continuance of our ministry. The bones also helped guard our monastery from the greed of King Dúnlaing's nobles. Without them, I'm certain they will press the king to take back our land."

I nodded in agreement. As bad as things had seemed for our monastery a week ago, they were considerably worse now.

"But I didn't call you here, Sister Deirdre, to explain the dire circumstances we face. You know them as well as I. The simple fact is we must find those bones before the beginning of spring or our monastery is finished. The feast day of holy Brigid in early February, just over three months from now, draws more pilgrims to our community than any event of the year. If we can't recover the bones by then, our ministry, our monastery, our dream is over."

No matter how much I might wish it otherwise, what she said was true.

"We've searched and questioned everyone around the monastery to no avail, not that I'm surprised. I find it most unlikely that one of our people would commit such an unholy crime against their own community. I can think of nothing anyone in the monastery would gain from the act. I can only assume, therefore, that the thief or thieves live beyond these walls."

I nodded in agreement.

"I'm so glad you concur, Sister Deirdre, because I am assigning you the task of finding the bones."

I looked at her in disbelief for several moments before I responded.

"You can't be serious. Me? Find the bones? A few days ago you said I was drifting like a ship at sea. Now you want to place the future of the monastery in my hands?"

"I appreciate the irony as well, Sister Deirdre, but be quiet and listen. You wouldn't be my choice for the task under different circumstances, but whoever has taken the bones of holy Brigid must come from outside this community, perhaps from beyond the bounds of these tribal lands. We both know that the only people who can move freely between tribes are members of the nobility such as yourself. You are a bard, a member of the Order of Druids. If it were up to me, I would question every person on this island myself to find those bones, but I'm not a warrior, a druid, a king, or one of the privileged few as you are. Even a blacksmith can wander the land and cross its tribal borders without the permission of a king, but the abbess of Kildare cannot."

I had never given any thought to this benefit of being part of the Irish nobility. It was simply part of my birthright.

"In addition to your ability to travel, you have many friends throughout the four provinces of Ireland. Your work as a bard has gained you influence with kings and commoners alike. You come from a family of druids and have a bond to members of the Order in every tribe. I leave aside the fact that you are insufferably curious. If anyone of the community of Brigid can find those bones, it's you."

"But, Sister Anna, where should I look? Who would have dared such a thing, even those living beyond these walls?"

"That, Sister Deirdre, I leave for you to discover. You will never find the bones by searching under rocks or beds. They could be safely hidden anywhere by now. So I would suggest you begin by asking yourself who had something to gain from such a theft. Question people. Use your connections. The bones were not carried off by spirits. Someone must have seen something. Someone must know something. Find that person."

She then reached under her desk and handed me the small wooden box containing the silk ribbon from Brigid's chest and the piece of cloth the armed stranger had left behind on Tamun's farm.

"Take these. They may be helpful, though I doubt it. But for now they're the only clues we have."

She nodded towards the door.

"You are released from all other duties at the monastery during this task. What meager resources we have are at your disposal. Go now, and may the grace of God go with you."

I bowed my head to leave, but suddenly thought of something.

"Sister Anna, may Sister Darerca help me search for the bones? She could be helpful. She sees things I don't."

Sister Anna waved me away.

"Yes, fine. I can scarcely separate the two of you anyway."

I bowed again and went out, almost forgetting to close the door behind me. I was terrified. How could I find such a small bundle of bones? It seemed like an impossible job and I had no idea where to begin.

Who had something to gain from stealing the bones? I first went to the church and prayed. After that I talked briefly with Brother Kevin, who was outside the carpenter's shop. Then to help me think, I went back to the sleeping quarters and retrieved my harp. Normally I would have gone straight to Father Ailbe's hut and poured my heart out to him, but it would be at least a week until he returned from Munster.

I set off on a path leading through the fields south of the monastery. When I reached a small rise, I looked back at Kildare and could see the church shining in the sun. It was perhaps a hundred feet long and half again as wide. I'm sure it was nothing compared to the churches in Rome or Constantinople that Father Ailbe had visited, but since I was a little girl it seemed like the grandest building in the world to me. It was made from solid oak boards fixed against an oak frame and painted with a lime whitewash. Even the roof was made of overlapping oak planks. The oak tree was sacred to the druids, but it was perfectly permissible to build with it. It was the most sturdy of woods and naturally resistant to rot. The monastery took its name from the church, built by Brigid when she had first established the settlement fifty years earlier. She had wanted to name it for the Virgin Mary, but from the start people had called it *Cill Dara* or Kildare—"The Church of Oak"—and the name stuck.

"Admiring the view, Deirdre?"

I turned and saw Roech, a nobleman of King Dúnlaing. Roech owned the land to the south of the monastery and was a close friend of Dúnlaing's sons Illann and Ailill. He was also a cousin of mine on my father's side. He was a lean man with a bulbous nose who loved hunting, gambling, and bedding as many women as he could threaten or buy. I grew up thinking he was a disgusting lout and hadn't found any reason to change my mind.

"Yes, Roech, I'm admiring Brigid's church. A shining beacon of holiness to those who dwell in its shadow, don't you think?"

He snorted.

"Holiness is for women and fools. A man's business is to fight for his king, increase his herds, and sleep with a different wench every night—two if he can find them."

He laughed at his own joke. I was unimpressed.

"Well, Deirdre, in any case it sounds like your church won't be around much longer. With the bones of Brigid gone missing and, I hear, a certain church across the Barrow burned to the ground, I think King Dúnlaing will be taking back his lands soon enough. Such a pity. I always enjoyed hearing you nuns sing as I walked by."

"And what would you know about the missing bones, Roech?"

A silk ribbon only a nobleman could afford. A warrior running away in the darkness. The clues so far pointed to a man like Roech, especially one who had always despised Brigid and her monastery. If we couldn't pay our rent to the king and lost our lands, Roech stood to benefit greatly.

I leaned in close and fixed him with an icy stare. It was a trick I had learned from my grandmother to throw a man off balance. He jerked back and almost fell down.

"I don't know anything about your moldy old bones. I'd grind them into meal to feed my pigs if I could find them. Brigid never did me any favors."

Roech had once tried to blackmail a beautiful young woman into sleeping with him after entrusting a valuable brooch to her father for safekeeping. He sent one of his own men to secretly steal it in the night, then said that if the brooch wasn't returned to him in three days he would take the man's daughter as his slave in payment. The family was frantic and came to Brigid for help. She prayed with them, then went to see one of Roech's shepherds whose wife she had once healed. He finally told her what his master had done and where he had hidden the brooch. When the day came for Roech to claim the girl as his slave, Brigid was there at her family's home and handed the brooch to him with a smile. Roech stormed away cursing Brigid for meddling in his business.

"Oh, such an unfortunate attitude, Roech. I'm sure Brigid is praying for you even now as she looks down upon you from heaven."

He glanced up quickly, then back at me.

"Spare me your Christian prayers, Deirdre. I don't need you or Brigid to help me. Things are changing, you see. Things are going to be different soon."

Roech acted like a small man with a big secret. He was probably just bluffing, but something in his words made me wonder.

"What do you mean things will be different soon?"

He seemed to realize he had said too much.

"Nothing. I mean nothing."

Before he could walk away, I moved in front of him and addressed him in the formal manner of a bard.

"Roech, son of Lóeg, as a bard of the ancient line of Amairgen, I call on you to tell me what you know. If you fail to do so, I will curse you with the power of my druid blood and the magic of women."

He began to shake and back away as I continued, one palm stretched out toward him and the other raised to the sky.

"You will be enchanted and bound. The great will become small, the straight will be crooked, the seeing will be blind. Your fields will bear no fruit, your cows no calves, your women no children. Your bounty and your manhood will shrivel like a bean left on the stalk in winter. You will die without a name and be forgotten."

He screamed and turned to run, shouting behind him as he fled.

"I know nothing! I know nothing!"

Sometimes it was fun to be a druid.

But now I was worried. If Roech knew of some plot to ruin the monastery, that probably meant King Dúnlaing's sons were involved. They had been scheming for years to take back the lands of the monastery, though Roech's cocky tone made me think that this time it was something more.

Chapter Five

I walked for half an hour past Roech's farm to a small spring-fed well. It was the most peaceful place I knew and I had often come here in the past to think when I was troubled. It had been a holy place for women since ages past and was still frequented by those seeking help or healing.

There beneath a canopy of trees was an altar dedicated to a goddess whose name was long forgotten. Visitors would often leave an offering or tie a piece of cloth to the tree above the well as a kind of prayer. Brigid herself had come many times. When I was a girl, I once asked her how she could pray at a pagan shrine, but she only smiled and said the whole world was sacred to God in heaven. After she died, so many Christian women had begun to visit the place that soon it became known as Brigid's Well. There was even a small stone cross next to the altar of the goddess.

The water from the spring flowed into a creek that I followed to the home of my grandmother. She was a wise woman of sound advice, though I didn't listen to it often enough. Her house was in a clearing surrounded by oak trees beneath a small hill. Although it was off the main road, there had been a constant stream of visitors to her door for as long as I could remember. Like her mother and her mother's mother before her back to the beginning of time, I suppose, my grandmother was a druid skilled in prophesy and visions. She also had more common sense than anyone I had ever met, with the possible exception of Brigid. Often when someone came to her looking for answers, she didn't even need to sacrifice the chicken or rabbit they had brought. She would just sit down and talk with them, listening carefully to what they said and didn't say, then tell them what they should do. People were so grateful for her help that she developed a reputation all over the island as a great seer. She travelled frequently around Leinster and the other provinces to preside at rituals of birth, marriage, and death, often with me beside her before I became a nun.

I had lived with her in that house from the time I was an infant until I got married. My father had died just before I was born while he was fighting with King Dúnlaing against the Uí Néill along the Boyne River. My mother had moved back home with me after his death even though she and my grandmother often argued. She had dark red hair like me and was beautiful enough to attract suitors from the whole province after my father died. She sent them all away so that she could live a quiet life on our farm with no man to rule over her.

I wish I could remember my mother better. I have an image of her in my mind holding me in her arms and telling me stories before I fell asleep. I also remember her holding my hand as we walked through the wet spring grass to look at flowers. But mostly I remember her and my grandmother arguing.

Much to the annoyance of my grandmother, my mother never had any interest in being a druid. To make matters worse, she had become a devout Christian as a teenager and attended worship regularly at the monastery. I had been baptized there and later instructed in the faith by Father Ailbe and the sisters of Kildare. My mother had died of a fever just before my fourth birthday. On her deathbed, she made my grandmother promise to raise me as a Christian. To her credit, my grandmother kept her vow and didn't try to turn me away from the faith.

As I approached the home I had lived in for so long, I saw the smoke coming from the hole in the center of the thatched roof and smelled roasted chicken, my favorite dish. I knocked on the door, then entered the cozy hut. My old bed was on the right, while my grandmother's was at the far end of the single room. There were dried herbs and a smoked ham hanging from one of the rafters. The cooking cauldron was at the center of the hut over the fire and next to it was my grandmother.

"Well, look who's come to visit at last. I thought I would die alone some cold, dark night without ever again seeing the face of my only granddaughter."

I kissed her on the cheek and took off my cloak.

"Grandmother, it's only been two weeks since I was here. You know I would have come sooner but I was across the Barrow River at Sleaty."

"Yes, I heard about the church. But it seems to me you have greater troubles now, since Anna has put you in charge of finding Brigid's bones."

I looked at her in surprise. She was shorter than me, barely up to my shoulders. Although as healthy as a yearling horse, she was over seventy now, with silver hair and a mischievous twinkle in her eye.

"Is there anything you don't know? I met with Sister Anna just this morning."

"Oh, my dear, the spirits tell me many things. I also spoke with Brother Kevin a little while ago when he stopped by. He filled me in on everything."

I remember a family friend once said that the secret to being a successful seer was to be an irrepressible gossip.

"What am I going to do, Grandmother? Those bones could be anywhere by now."

"The first thing you're going to do is have some supper. I know the monastery has fallen on hard times, but I don't think they're feeding you enough. You're as skinny as a newborn calf. Come help me with dinner."

It was good to be busy while we talked. Conversation is so much easier when you have something to do with your hands. The main meal in my grandmother's house was always eaten in the afternoon, as in most homes. Our food was simple, mostly bread, butter, cheese, and milk, sometimes mixed into a porridge. We ate meat more often in the winter, usually chicken or salted pork, but it was not a large part of our diet until after the first frost. My grandmother made a wonderful relish of garden vegetables and honey that we always ate with our bread.

That afternoon, I churned the cream to separate the butter from the buttermilk, then strained, washed, and pressed it while my grandmother prepared the loaves.

No one could make bread like my grandmother. The day before she had dissolved a pinch of yeast in warm water and mixed it with a handful of barley flour for leavening. She kneaded it briefly, then shaped it into a ball. She placed this leavening into an earthenware pot and pressed her thumb on top of it to make a small indentation, then poured water into the hole. After this she covered the leavening with a lid and let it ferment in a warm place near the hearth until the next day.

When I arrived, she went to her pantry and brought out a large jar of barley flour as well as her precious supply of fine flour made from wheat, a difficult grain to grow properly in cool, wet Ireland. When offered a cow or gold for her services as a druid seer, she would often request wheat flour instead. She told me one milk cow was enough for an old lady living alone and that good bread flour was more precious to her than gold.

She had sifted the wheat and barley flour together in equal amounts with warm water, then placed the dough on a wooden board to work. After she had kneaded it, she worked in the leavening and put it into a clay pot to rise. The smell of yeast soon filled the air.

When I had finished with the butter, I pulled the silk ribbon out of my pocket.

"Grandmother, whoever stole the bones replaced the ribbon on the chest with this."

She wiped the flour off her hands and took the ribbon from me, holding it up to the light streaming in through her window to examine it closely.

"Silk, the best quality too. Whoever the thief was has good taste." she said.

"Can you sense anything from it?"

She held it in the flat of her palm as she looked at it closely.

"Strange," she said. "All I sense from this is sadness."

"But can you tell anything about the thief from it?"

"No, it does narrow down the suspects considerably though. Only a member of the nobility could afford this."

"Sister Anna and I thought so too. What about this?"

I handed her the piece of tartan cloth. She studied it for a minute.

"A Leinster weave, though I'm not sure about the pattern. It looks like one of the clans on the southern edge of Dúnlaing's kingdom or maybe across the border in the Wicklow Mountains. Where did you get it?"

"From a hawthorn tree on Tamun's farm. He chased a warrior away with a hoe on Michaelmas evening."

"That sounds like Tamun."

She held it as she had the silk ribbon and closed her eyes. "Hmm. A tall man, dark hair, confident, loyal."

"Grandmother, that describes half the warriors in Ireland."

"True, but you don't know the owner was connected to the theft of the bones in any case, though it is strange to have someone like that skulking around the monastery."

I left my grandmother while the dough was rising and went outside to feed her chickens. Then I walked down to a small grove behind the hut and picked a basket of wild apples for her. These were small sour fruits unlike the sweet red apples we grew at the monastery, but they were quite tasty when dried and sprinkled with honey.

I put the apples in her pantry and sat down on the bench near her.

"Grandmother, do you have any idea who might have taken the bones?"

"No, but perhaps you do."

"What do you mean? If I knew who took them I wouldn't be here having dinner."

"I mean that you're a smart girl. Think about who has something to gain from taking them."

"That's the same thing Sister Anna said."

"A wise woman, for a Christian."

Grandmother was actually on very good terms with Sister Anna and the rest of the members of the monastery in spite of her aversion to our religion. She and Father Ailbe were fond of each other as well, which pleased me greatly.

"At least I know that whoever took the bones couldn't have been a Christian," I said. "A believer would see them as sacred objects. It would be like defiling the Eucharist or cursing God to his face."

"My child, I think you have too much faith in the presumed goodness of Christians. I've known many of your faith in my time, some of whom I wouldn't trust to milk my cow. Don't you remember that Christian King Coroticus from Britain back in Patrick's day who kidnapped all the young Irish women in Ulster and sold them into slavery?"

"And Patrick roundly condemned him for it," I countered. "He wrote him a scathing letter threatening the wrath of God on him and his men if they didn't return them."

"So, did he bring the women back?"

"No." I sighed. "Coroticus said he was within his rights as a king to do whatever he wanted in Ireland. He also got the British bishops to support him."

"My point exactly. Anyone can justify their actions to themselves if they want something badly enough. So don't cross the Christians off your list of suspects."

"But Grandmother, Coroticus was an exception. He wasn't a true Christian, even Patrick said so."

"Don't lecture me about Patrick, young lady. I knew him long before you were born. He wasn't bad looking, even in his later years, with piercing blue eyes and a thick head of wavy hair. You know, if I hadn't been with your grandfather, I would have taken him back to my hut and showed him my—"

"Grandmother!"

"Oh peace, child," she chuckled. "Patrick had his faults— a bit moody at times and a fierce temper when you crossed him—but he was sincere in his strange devotion to celibacy, in spite of my considerable charms in those days."

She laughed again and sashayed across the floor to the hearth like a young maiden at a spring dance.

Now that the dough had risen, she shaped it into two loaves and placed them over the coals of the hearth with a heated brick above them to make sure the baking would be even.

41

"Grandmother, do you think druids could be involved?"

"I seriously doubt it, my dear. The druids always respected Brigid and her work. There are a few malcontents who feel threatened by your faith, but our way is always open to new ideas. Some of your Christian stories are actually similar to our own. I always thought your Jesus would have made a fine druid if he'd been fortunate enough to have been born Irish."

She basted the chicken as I continued.

"But what Christian would do such a thing?"

"I'm not saying your thief was necessarily a Christian, Deirdre. It's just that you have to consider the possibility. There are other Christian groups in Ireland besides the followers of Brigid, like the monks at Armagh. They could be behind the missing bones. They're one of the largest landholders in Ulster and have plenty of gold. Their abbot—a vile little man—probably has a whole drawer full of silk ribbons. They've always resented Brigid's monastery as a rival to their own power and would love to destroy it. If they didn't steal the bones themselves, they could have hired someone to do it for them."

She went out to the barn to feed her cow while I cleared off the table and brought out some plates. When she came back, I asked her who else she thought could have taken the bones.

"My money would be on King Dúnlaing's men, maybe even his sons," she said. "They would profit greatly from seizing the monastery lands. I know the king himself would condemn the theft, but if one of his men, especially one with lands near the monastery, thought he could serve his own interests by stealing them, it wouldn't be hard for him to slip in and out of the church one night with nobody the wiser."

"I saw Roech on the way here, Grandmother. He acted like he knew something I didn't."

"Roech is an idiot. You need to talk to Dúnlaing himself."

"And what am I supposed to do? March into the king's feasting hall and ask him if any of his men stole the bones of Brigid?"

"Why not? You're a bard. Threaten him with satire if he doesn't turn over the thief."

"And if he decides to cut my head off instead?"

"Then he'll owe me twenty cows as your next of kin."

We both laughed. No king would dare lay hands on a bard.

The bread was starting to smell wonderful. I could tell it was almost done.

"Grandmother, there's something else, though it's probably nothing."

"And what would that be, my child?"

"Last night, just as I was falling asleep, I thought I heard a voice speaking to me."

My grandmother suddenly looked very serious.

"What kind of voice? What did it say?"

"Well, it was an old woman, a voice I didn't recognize. She told me to return to the fire, whatever that means. But honestly, I probably just dreamed it. I feel silly even mentioning it to you."

My grandmother put down the pot she was washing and sat next to me.

"Deirdre, my love, never dismiss the power of dreams or voices in the night. That's how the spirits most often speak to us. Give me your hand and say the words again."

She took my right hand in hers and closed her eyes. I repeated the words of the old woman slowly several times while my grandmother mumbled something I didn't understand. Finally she opened her eyes and spoke.

"The fire she spoke of is the church at Sleaty. Something happened there that isn't right, isn't what it seems to be."

"Why? What do you see?"

"The images are dim, like shadows. I see someone watching you as you sleep, looking down on you, full of hatred, coming near. He isn't alone, others are outside. I see fire, a candle against fresh wood, flames growing. Someone was there with you in the church. Someone who set the fire. Someone who wanted to kill you."

"Grandmother, that's not possible. I was the one who burned down the church at Sleaty. There wasn't anyone else there."

"Are you sure?"

"Well, I think so. I mean, I didn't see anyone else, though I thought I heard something outside at one point. I suppose someone could have snuck in quietly while I slept. I was very tired."

"Deirdre, you've got to listen to that voice. Someone else burned down the church, not you. Someone who wanted to kill you as well as destroy the church. You've got to go back to Sleaty and find out."

"But how? What would I look for in a pile of charred ruins?"

"I don't know, but there must be something there or the voice wouldn't be urging you to return."

I sat beside my grandmother for several minutes taking everything in. Could I really be innocent of starting the fire at Sleaty? Would anyone believe me if I claimed I didn't? I couldn't very well say I heard a voice in a dream that said I wasn't guilty. No one would believe me. I didn't really believe it myself. I needed proof before I could talk to Sister Anna. And who would want me dead?

"Grandmother, I can think of a few people on this island who don't like me, but I can't think of anyone who would actually want to kill me. Am I in danger?"

She shook her head.

"I don't think so, at least not at the moment. The feeling I got was that whoever burned down the church wasn't expecting to find you there. It was more of a sudden rage, some deep anger that seeing you provoked. But you have to be careful. Whoever set the fire at Sleaty might try to kill you outright next time, especially if he knows you suspect him."

"But who would want to burn down the church?"

"Who would want to steal the bones? If you can answer the first question it might help you with the second. Maybe the two are related."

As she said this, she rose and took the bread from the hearth. Underneath the brick were two perfect loaves with a soft crust on top. In spite of my new worries, my mouth began to water. I took some of the butter and placed it in a dish for both of us. If there is something closer to heaven in this world than my grandmother's hot bread with fresh butter and honey relish on top, I don't know what it is.

"But enough talk about churches and bones." My grandmother pointed me to the table. "Come sit down and have some chicken. You can't save the world on an empty stomach."

Chapter Six

At the monastery the next evening, I helped with the cooking and cleaning up after dinner. We fed all the sisters and our handful of brothers at each meal along with the twenty or so widows who lived with us. I collected the table scraps and went out to feed the pigs in the pen at the far end of the compound. We were fattening them for slaughter soon and so had brought them in from the woods a few weeks earlier. Tending pigs was the job of slaves in most places, but Brigid had taught us that even the most humble task was of value when done in the service of God.

Our pigs were small hairy animals with long legs, barely distinguishable from the wild boars that roamed the forest. Most were black or reddish-brown, but the largest sow was white with red ears. I sat down on the log bench next to their pen.

When I was a girl, I used to marvel at the way Brigid had with animals, including pigs. One autumn afternoon when she was helping to bring the monastery swine into the feeding pen, a large wild boar suddenly burst into the middle of the herd. The poor animal had been running away from something and was as surprised as the sisters to find itself surrounded by strange pigs. It started to panic and charge around the herd, then Brigid began to walk slowly toward it, singing gently. She motioned to the other sisters to stand still as she approached the boar. They were terrified the beast would gore her with its sharp tusks, but as she came ever closer it seemed to calm down. At last Brigid knelt beside it and stroked its back as she whispered into its ear. Then she led it out of the herd and back into the forest.

The pigs in the pen that chilly night were all healthy and happy as they devoured the scraps I had brought them from the kitchen. Soon they would be ready to be made into sausage and hams to feed us, hopefully, through the winter. I always felt guilty about killing pigs even though I enjoyed their sweet meat. They are intelligent creatures, more so than some people I've known. It never bothered me to wring a chicken's neck, but pigs were different.

I heard heavy footsteps coming toward me in the darkness and stood up. I grabbed a large stick resting against the pig pen, ready to defend myself against anyone trying to kill me as they had at the Sleaty fire, at least according to my grandmother. The full moon had risen, but thick clouds covered the sky. I strained to see who was coming, then a familiar deep voice spoke to me.

"Still fond of pigs, are you, Deirdre?"

It was Fergus, my ex-husband. I lowered the stick, but kept it in my hand.

"What are you doing here, Fergus?"

"I was passing through. I was doing some cattle trading nearby and decided to stop in. Do I need a reason to visit my wife?"

"I'm not your wife anymore, as you well know."

"I know I always treated you well enough. I didn't hit you often and I think I satisfied you, if you know what I mean. I could go to the brehons and get a judgment against you if I wanted."

"Go ahead and try. Most of them are my cousins."

Fergus sighed and shrugged.

"Deirdre, why do you always have to be so difficult? Was I really such a bad husband? Life on my farm couldn't have been that bad. Ness and Boann miss you. So do their children."

"How are they doing? Has Tiger learned to shoot a bow yet?"

"You should see him. The boy can bring down a deer at a hundred paces now. We went hunting last week and he killed the largest buck I've ever seen. We had a great feast when we got home and smoked the rest for winter. Did you know Ness had a son at the end of last month and Boann twin daughters just a couple of weeks ago?"

"Yes, I heard."

"There are so many crying babies around the place I can't get a good night's sleep anymore."

"The burdens of fatherhood, Fergus."

"Oh, mind you, I'm not complaining. What more could a man want than a house full of children?"

This talk about children with Fergus was becoming painful.

"Fergus, why are you here?"

He walked over and sat on the bench. I stood facing him.

"I heard about the bones. I also heard about what happened at Sleaty. Are you alright?"

"Just a few scrapes. Nothing to worry about."

I knew he hadn't come all the way to the monastery to make sure I was well. He wanted something.

"Deirdre," he said at last, "I don't want you to think I'm trying to take advantage of a bad situation, but with the monastery in trouble, I wanted to let you know you're always welcome to come back home and live with me, if you want to."

I was as likely to move back in with Fergus as become a Frankish concubine.

"Fergus, honestly, why would you want me back? You and I fought all the time."

"Oh, I suppose I like a challenge. It's like having a feisty heifer that won't let a bull mount her."

"You really know how to flatter a girl, Fergus."

"You know what I mean. I miss you, Deirdre. My other wives are good women, but they're not like you. Sometimes after spending an evening with you I wanted to pound my head against the wall, but life was always interesting when you were around."

He reached down to tie the lace on his boot.

"I guess I'm trying to say I love you. I always will."

Fergus had never spoken to me like this before, even when we were married, and I wasn't sure I believed him.

"Fergus, I'm touched, but I'm not looking for a husband. I'm a nun now and my life is here at the monastery."

I took a deep breath.

"And besides, you know why I left."

Memories came flooding back like it was yesterday. His shining eyes and sweet laughter, rocking him to sleep in my arms as we sat by the fire.

"I loved him too, Deirdre. I was his father, you know. You don't own all the grief."

I was not going to do this. I was not going to fight with Fergus. I was not going to talk about my son.

"Fergus, this is my home now. Please leave."

"But you can't stay here, Deirdre. You know the monastery won't survive without Brigid's bones."

"I'm hoping to find them before it's too late. If not, I'll make my own way somehow."

He stood up and faced me.

"Maybe I could help. If I could find the bones for you, would you think about coming back to me?"

I suddenly wondered if Fergus might be the thief. If he wanted to ruin the monastery or blackmail me into returning to him, stealing the bones would be a good way to do it.

"And just how could you find them, Fergus?"

"I deal with a lot of people in the livestock business, some of them pretty shady characters. They might know something. I could ask around."

I had to be careful how I handled this. If he was the thief, taking a tough stand with him would be better than appearing weak.

"I'm sorry, Fergus. I'd be grateful if you let me know of anything you might hear, but I'm afraid our marriage is over, forever."

He stood facing me with a look of fury on his face. At first I thought he was going to hit me with those meaty fists of his and I gripped my stick tightly, but I watched as he made himself calm down.

"You might feel differently this winter when the wind blows down from the north. I know you can always go back to living with your grandmother, but not everyone has a cozy fire waiting for them. Maybe you could take Father Ailbe and Dari with you, but what about the other sisters and brothers? What about all those widows you feed? Can you squeeze everyone into her hut? It's going to get pretty crowded."

"We'll survive," I said. "Goodbye, Fergus."

He grumbled something and left out of the back gate of the monastery. I didn't believe for a minute that he'd come to declare his love for me. I also didn't think he was bright enough to come up with the idea of stealing the bones himself. He'd struggled at the monastery school for a few years and could manage basic reading and writing, but he'd quit when his father said he didn't have to go anymore. Could he be working for someone else? If so, who? And why was he trying so hard to get me to come back to his farm now, three years after I left him? I knew it wasn't out of concern for me. There was something more going on with Fergus than he was admitting and I was determined to discover what it was.

Chapter Seven

I was late the next day for morning prayers. I walked quickly into the church and stood in back, hoping nobody would notice. The other nuns were lined up in front of me facing the altar with their veils over their heads. A couple of the older sisters seemed so shaky I could have knocked them over with a feather. The brothers standing on the other side of the church seemed just as despondent. It felt as if we were all attending a funeral. The theft of the bones was wearing deeply on everyone.

That morning's first psalm was a perfect match for the mood. The sisters began the melodic chant:

> *Have mercy on me, O Lord,*
> *for I am in distress.*
> *Tears have wasted my eyes,*
> *my throat and my heart.*

Then the brothers took over:

For my life is spent with sorrow,
and my years with sighs.
Affliction has broken down my strength,
and my bones waste away.

I was glad we used the psalms in our prayer services. There are a hundred and fifty of them covering every human emotion from boundless joy to abject despair. Sing them all in a few weeks and you're bound to find one that fits. I also like them because I'm not good at coming up with my own prayers. I can compose a lengthy eulogy for a king at a moment's notice, but a prayer from the heart is different. Sometimes it seemed silly to me to talk to God since he already knows what we need and he never talks back. But Father Ailbe always said that prayer is for our own benefit.

The sisters finished the last refrain:

Be strong, let your heart take courage,
all who hope in the Lord.

As the others filed out at the end of the service to make their way to the dining hut for breakfast, Sister Anna motioned for me to stay behind. I stood by the door waiting for her to yell at me.

"Sister Anna, I'm sorry I was late. I couldn't find my—"

"Spare me, Sister Deirdre. Come to my office after you eat. I have something for you."

She left the church quickly, heading to her hut. She normally ate breakfast alone at her desk. I joined the rest of the brothers and sisters in the dining hall. They were having our usual morning meal of bread and milk, though I noticed the butter jar was none too full. Dari had already taken her meal to the school to eat with the children. I sat down at a table but none of the others seemed like they wanted to talk to me. They all avoided my eyes. Only Eithne whispered to me.

"Has Sister Anna really put you in charge of finding the bones?"

"Yes."

"Then God help us. The monastery is doomed."

I waited for one of the others to come to my defense, but they either hadn't heard or they agreed with Eithne. Many of them were still angry at me for the fire at Sleaty. I wanted to tell them that a mysterious voice had spoken to me about the fire and that my grandmother had said it wasn't my fault, but that would have sounded pathetic. My only hope for redemption was to find proof that someone else had burned down the church.

When I had finished eating I walked to the hut of the abbess and knocked on her door.

"Come in."

Sister Anna was working at her desk. She motioned me towards her and handed me a small piece of parchment carefully folded and sealed with a circle of yellow wax. My name was written in Roman letters on the front.

"This was brought by a messenger last night."

The image pressed into the wax seal was of a striking young man in profile with a ram's horn curling over his ear. I realized that it was made by an old coin of Alexander the Great. Father Ailbe had one like it in the chest he had brought from Egypt.

I broke the seal and saw that the writing was in Greek:

> Deirdre,
> I thought it best to write in a language few know in case
> this letter is intercepted. You must come to my inaugura-

*tion at Glendalough. I have information about the bones
of Brigid.*

Cormac

*P.S. Isn't the seal wonderful? I had it made from a
golden coin I got from an Italian merchant. It cost me
three slaves, but it was worth it.*

Cormac. I felt my heart stop as I read his name. I hadn't
seen or heard from him in several years, not since just before
I married Fergus. He had sent me a wedding gift then, a fine
Roman oil lamp with an image of the lovers Pyramus and
Thisbe carved on top.

I handed the letter to Sister Anna, who glanced at it briefly.

"Well, what does it say?" she asked.

The abbess didn't know Greek, though she was quite good
at Latin. There weren't more than a handful of people in
Ireland who could write in Greek and they were all former
students of Father Ailbe. He had also taught me Aramaic, the
language of Jesus, and a little Hebrew, though I struggled
with the latter.

"It's from Cormac. He wants me to go to Glendalough for
his inauguration. He says he has information regarding the
bones of Brigid."

"Indeed? What kind of information?"

"He doesn't say."

"I find it rather odd that Cormac sends us word about the
bones so soon after they're stolen."

So did I. Could Cormac be involved in the theft of Brigid's
bones? I didn't want to believe it. Maybe he just wanted to see
me again. It had been so long.

"Sister Anna, you don't think he might have taken the bones,
do you?"

"Possibly. Cormac is an ambitious man. If stealing them would serve his quest for power, then yes, I think he could be behind it."

"But he was a student here for years. He's practically a member of our community," I protested.

"A student, yes, but he never received baptism. If Cormac believes in anything beyond his own destiny I would be very much surprised."

"Sister Anna, I admit that Cormac is perfectly capable of bold action to further his ambitions, but I don't see how having the bones would help him."

"Neither do I. Perhaps he has truly heard something. Perhaps he is using the news of the theft for his own purposes. But if he has the bones, you must get them back."

She tapped her fingers on her desk for a moment. I could tell she was weighing something in her mind.

"Sister Deirdre, I'm reluctant to send you to Glendalough alone."

I could feel myself blushing. Sister Anna knew about Cormac and me. She had been one of our teachers when he and I were in school together and she seldom missed anything. I don't know if she knew about our nighttime meetings, but I wouldn't have been surprised.

"I'm afraid I must insist that Sister Darerca accompany you."

I was glad to have Dari come along, but I was indignant at having her appointed to watch over me.

"Sister Anna, I assure you that Cormac is part of my past. With respect, I don't need a chaperone."

"I disagree, and fortunately I am the one who gets to make such decisions. In any case, I'm not worried about your virtue as much as I am your objectivity."

"Yes, Sister Anna." I bit my lip. One did not argue with the abbess of Kildare.

"Now, aside from the dubious promise of information from young Cormac, tell me what you have found so far in your search and how you plan to proceed."

I wasn't going to tell her about the voice of the old woman in the night unless I found something at Sleaty. It also seemed best not to mention my suspicions of Fergus until I found out more.

"Well, I'm afraid I can't tell you anything definite, though I have several ideas about who I should question. It still seems to me the primary suspects are the nobles of King Dúnlaing, especially his two sons, Illann and Ailill. They have a strong motivation for wanting to ruin us and take back the lands of Kildare for themselves. I don't think the king himself would be involved, but he's holding a Samain feast at Dún Ailinne next week and all his nobles will be there. I'd like to go and see what I can find out."

Sister Anna nodded.

"Who else will you question?"

"I plan to visit some farmsteads southwest of Kildare before I visit the king. I'll leave tomorrow. We haven't had a chance to question everyone there yet."

Actually I had no intention of talking to any farmers. I was using it as an excuse to revisit Sleaty and examine the ruined church.

"Who else?"

"It's possible some disgruntled druids may be behind the theft."

Sister Anna frowned.

"The Order always respected Brigid. Our relations with them have been amicable since her death. I find it unlikely that they would be involved."

"That's what my grandmother said."

"A wise woman, for a druid."

"Then there's the monastery of Armagh," I continued. "The abbot there has been trying to undermine us for years. If he had his way we would all be declared heretics and excommunicated. He has the backing of a few of the Irish bishops and even some support in Rome. But I can't bring myself to believe he would steal the bones of Brigid. Sister Anna, you've met the abbot a number of times. May I ask what you think of him?"

"I think that the abbot would sell his mother to a Pictish brothel if it would increase his power. I hate to think that a man who calls himself a Christian would commit such a blasphemy as to steal the bones of holy Brigid, but it is possible. Still, he would never have his own men do the deed. It would be too obvious. He would work through someone else."

"Outlaws?"

"Possibly. They've been known to commit such acts for the right price. Or perhaps he would use someone closer to Kildare. Someone who would raise fewer suspicions."

Just as I was about to ask Sister Anna who she had in mind, we heard the noise of horses outside. This was unusual, since the monastery owned none. Such animals were too expensive for us to feed and were kept mostly by the warrior nobility. My first thought was that it must be some of King Dúnlaing's nobles come to gloat over our misfortune.

But as we stepped out of the hut, I was surprised to see the riders were four men in monastic robes, though considerably finer than the ones we wore at Kildare. They all were tonsured in the Roman style with only the top of their heads shaved. The two largest monks wore fine swords strapped to their belts. The third was a man of average height who looked like a clerk with his ink-stained fingers. Like the large men, he wore a small silver cross about his neck on a silver chain. The fourth was a short, stout figure with delicate hands and no cross.

"Speak of the devil," said Sister Anna softly.

The abbot of Armagh had just ridden into our monastery.

Chapter Eight

G reetings, brothers and sisters in Christ."
The abbot spoke in an impressively booming voice
to the crowd that was gathering around.

One of the larger monks got down and helped the abbot slowly off his horse. He handed the reins to Brother Kevin without a word as if he were a stable boy. Then the abbot saw us and approached the abbess with arms outstretched.

"Sister Anna, my dear woman, what a pleasure it is to see you again."

He gripped Sister Anna's hands in his own as he talked.

"What a lovely little monastery you have here. I've been meaning to visit for so long but, as you well know, the demands of those of us who oversee the flocks of our Lord are great. Fortunately I was nearby supervising the completion of our new church at Clondalkin and I told myself I simply had to stop by."

The abbot of Armagh was the youngest son of an Uí Néill royal family and used the conquests of his kinsmen to the advantage of his monastery. He had established daughter churches in the lands conquered from us and was now trying to spread his influence into Munster and Leinster itself.

Sister Anna looked as if one of the Indian pythons Father Ailbe talked about had just slithered through our gate and wrapped itself around her. But she was nothing if not the proper host.

"Abbot, it's a pleasure to welcome you to Kildare. Please come inside my office so that you may rest after your long journey."

She pried herself loose from his grip and motioned him toward her door. She spoke to me quickly, telling me to bring refreshments from the kitchen. I scampered off and found the last of the buttermilk and poured it into a jar. I grabbed two clean cups and arranged a whole batch of Sister Brianna's honey cookies on our finest plate. I was determined to make as good an impression as possible on the abbot, though I hated to waste our food on him. I walked quickly back to Sister Anna's hut and knocked softly.

"Come in."

Sister Anna was at her desk while the abbot was smiling in the chair in front of her. His clerk was standing behind him looking as if he were afraid to touch anything.

"Abbot, this is Sister Deirdre, one of the newer members of our community. If you don't mind, I would like her to stay."

This was surprising, but I bowed to him with as much grace as I could muster. If Sister Anna was going to be polite, so could I.

"Ah yes, Sister Deirdre. It seems as if I've heard your name somewhere before. Weren't you a member of that horrible order of witches and sorcerers? I believe you were one of their singers, weren't you? I'm so glad you've seen the light of Christ and left behind those evil ways."

I felt the bile gathering in my throat, but before I could respond I caught the stern warning on Sister Anna's face. I measured my words carefully.

"Yes, Abbot, it is true I come from a family of druids and have been trained as a bard."

"Of course, of course," he said cheerfully. "I've heard you're very good with your harp. What a blessing that you now sing the praises of our Lord."

He then turned to Sister Anna with a most solemn expression.

"My dear Sister Anna, I cannot tell you how much it grieved me to hear about the loss of holy Brigid's bones. Unthinkable! I can't believe that someone would steal the bones of that blessed woman from her own church. Truly, we live in the last days if such crimes are committed in the heart of this wonderful Christian community."

"Thank you, Abbot. Your words are a comfort to us in our time of trial."

"Indeed, indeed," replied the abbot. He loved to repeat his words.

He took one of the cookies from the plate and began to nibble on it. He reminded me of a very large mouse.

"And it has also come to my unworthy ears that another tragedy has befallen your monastery recently. Is it true that your efforts to establish a church in Munster on the lands of King Bran have, as they say, gone up in flames?"

He glanced at me for just an instant as he said this.

"Yes, Abbot," Sister Anna answered, "The church at Sleaty was destroyed in an unfortunate fire."

"Oh, I am sorry, Sister Anna. It was such a promising idea. I passed by the site only a month ago on the way to Cashel to meet with King Feidelmid. I've been trying to persuade him to let us establish a church of our own in Munster. Your workmen at Sleaty were doing a splendid job. I know the poor souls there will be at a loss without the nuns of Kildare to minister to them. And of course, the grain from the fields there would have been a great benefit in your ministry here."

"Yes, it would have been helpful," Sister Anna conceded.

"Truly, truly. But perhaps your brothers at Armagh can be of service in your hour of need."

I watched Sister Anna's eyes narrow as the abbot continued.

"Our own supplies are meager in these hard times, but in the spirit of Christian fellowship we might be able to spare some food to help see you through the winter and into the next harvest. I fear the pilgrims who normally come to the festival of holy Brigid in February might not feel, shall we say, motivated to attend and bring their offerings this year without the bones to draw them. We would also be willing to pay the rent you owe King Dúnlaing and guarantee future payments as well. We may even be able to influence King Bran to allow the construction of a new church at Sleaty."

Sister Anna's expression didn't change.

"That is indeed most generous, Abbot."

He took another cookie and a long draft of the buttermilk.

"Of course, we would need to insist on a few conditions."

I could guess what was coming next.

"And what might those conditions be, Abbot?" asked Sister Anna.

"Nothing really. Mere trifles. To see that the resources we donate would be used prudently, I would need to appoint a few men to oversee their distribution. They would have to be stationed here at your monastery. I would also like to send a few priests to help in your spiritual mission. I believe Father Ailbe is the only ordained minister you have at present. May I ask where he is, by the way?"

"Father Ailbe has been visiting friends in the west," said Sister Anna. "He's making his way back to us even now."

"Oh, I'm so sorry I'll miss him. I hope he will be alright. So many things can happen on these wild roads. I never travel anywhere without my guards."

I was really starting to hate this man.

The abbot took two more cookies and passed his cup to Sister Anna for a refill of buttermilk.

"Father Ailbe is a such dear man," the abbot said. "I met him when he came to Armagh many years ago. I know he was a favorite disciple of our beloved Patrick."

This was an outrageous lie. Father Ailbe arrived in Ireland several years before Patrick. Although the two were friends, Father Ailbe was never his disciple. If anything, Patrick looked up to him as a teacher and guide.

Sister Anna spoke before I had a chance to cause any trouble.

"Yes, I'm sure Father Ailbe will regret missing you as well. As for your kind offer of help, I'm afraid I must decline. It would be unfair of us to take bread from the hungry mouths at Armagh to fill our own bellies. "

"Ah, I understand, Sister Anna." The abbot smiled in a most condescending way. "Well, do know that our offer remains open should you change your mind."

"Thank you, Abbot. We are still hopeful that we will recover the bones and be able to continue our ministry on our own. In fact, I have placed Sister Deirdre here in charge of searching for them. Perhaps you might have some counsel you could offer her. Your wisdom is renowned throughout the island."

I wondered why Sister Anna would tell him about me.

The abbot smiled again.

"Sister Deirdre seems a worthy choice to lead the investigation. My dear young lady, I wish you the very best in your search. I'm afraid any advice I could offer you would be superfluous. I can only say that I will keep you ever in my thoughts."

The abbot rose from his chair.

"Do you mind if I take a few of these cookies with me, Sister Anna? They are simply delicious."

"Of course, Abbot. Sister Brianna will be so pleased that you appreciate her baking."

The abbot handed the cookies to his clerk, who placed the entire batch, plate included, into his satchel. We then all went out the door into the muddy yard where the large brother helped the abbot back up onto his horse.

"Thank you so much for your kind hospitality, Sister Anna. I'll be heading back to Armagh now, but I hope you won't hesitate to send word if you need anything—or if you change your mind."

"You are most gracious, Abbot."

With a flick of his reins the abbot and his party rode swiftly out of the gate, splashing mud on those standing nearby. The crowd dispersed and returned to their work, leaving the abbess and me alone.

"Those cookies were meant for the children, Sister Anna."

"Yes, I know. But somehow I doubt the abbot would care."

"Now that you've seen him again, do you think he was responsible for the theft of the bones?"

"I think it is a distinct possibility."

"Then shouldn't we confront him? We could talk to Father Ailbe when he returns and force the abbot to tell us what he knows under threat of censure from the synod of bishops."

"No, we couldn't. The abbot is far too clever for that. The fact remains that we have no proof. Suspicion is not evidence. If he is responsible, I need you to find proof—solid proof."

"I will do my best, Sister Anna."

"I hope that will be enough. You see now how the vultures begin to circle. Even if the abbot isn't responsible for the theft of the bones, he is certainly quick to take advantage of the situation. Others will be as well. We have precious little time. You must find those bones."

Chapter Nine

D ari, did you pack the cheese?"
"Yes, Deirdre," she sighed. "Both the soft kind you
like so much and some of hard stuff. If we don't eat
the latter we can use it to fight off robbers. I got enough of both
from the kitchen to last us for a few days, plus some loaves of
bread we had left over from dinner."

Dari hadn't wanted to come on the trip back to the Sleaty
church with me. She rolled her eyes when I told her about the
dream. But I didn't want to go alone and at last I talked her into it.

After all the turmoil around the monastery since the theft
of the bones, it was restful to be walking through the Irish
countryside on a bright autumn day. The grasslands near the
monastery were full of flowering white and yellow daisies and
red clover. Cattle and sheep grazed in the meadows near scattered farmhouses and golden plovers whistled a plaintive cry
as they flew overhead.

After we had settled the matter of the cheese, Dari and I enjoyed the silence of the fields and forests for the next few hours, happy with each other's company and feeling no need to talk. We stopped for lunch near a small stream. A few clouds were moving in from the south and I feared we would have a storm before the day was over.

"Deirdre, exactly what are you hoping to find at Sleaty? It's been two weeks since the fire. There won't be any footprints left with all the rain we've had, and anything someone might have dropped would have been burned to a crisp in the fire. Did this mysterious voice give you any hints about what to look for?"

In spite of her deep faith in God, Dari was a very practical person who didn't believe in signs, wonders, or voices in the night. I knew she was going on this trip just to keep me happy.

"No, the voice didn't go into any details. Look, Dari, I feel as silly about all this as you do, but my grandmother is no fool. If she believes I should go back to Sleaty, that's what I'm going to do."

"Deirdre, you know I think the world of your grandmother, I just don't believe that dreams are a very good guide for how to live our lives."

"Normally I would agree, but I've been thinking about the voice I heard. I wonder if it was Brigid?"

Dari looked at me skeptically.

"So you think Brigid came back from the dead to whisper to you in your dreams?"

"I don't know, Dari. I know it sounds ridiculous, but if the fire at Sleaty is somehow tied to the missing bones then maybe she did."

Dari began packing our food back into her satchel.

"Well, if we're going to make it to the campsite before sunset we should get moving. I don't like the look of those clouds."

We walked for most of the afternoon along a low ridge and arrived at the forest glade where we had planned to spend the night just as the first cold raindrops began to hit us on the head. Dari looked at the sky and frowned.

"Our tarp isn't going to do us much good if the wind picks up. You know, Deirdre, there is a dry place nearby where we could spend the night."

"Dari, no, please. I don't want to stay with Tuán. I'd rather get wet here in the woods."

"You're going to get soaked here in the woods and so am I. Come on, Tuán isn't so bad. At least his hut is warm and dry."

By now the rain was starting to fall harder. In a moment of weakness, I agreed, and so we set off down a side trail into the woods.

Tuán was an old monk who lived alone in a small hermitage in the nearby forest. He had been there as long as anyone, even Father Ailbe, could remember. He came to the monastery every few months to bring us honey, beeswax, and fresh mead. He made the mead himself from the honey he cultivated in dozens of hives around his hut. The wax he brought was essential for making votive candles and the writing tablets we used in our school. Like Brigid, he had an extraordinary gift for working with animals. I had been to his home only once before and had marveled at the ravens, squirrels, and hares that followed him around his little glen. He was a genius at taming wild creatures. He was also completely mad.

It was almost dark when we came to Tuán's home. He was outside, feeding by hand the largest deer I had ever seen. The animal almost bolted when it saw us, but Tuán whispered something in its ear and it quickly calmed down.

"Sisters, welcome!" He grabbed our arms and began to pull us towards his hut. "The birds told me you were on your way. Come inside and put your things on my guest bed. I've got a stew cooking over the fire and fresh bread on the coals. You must have a cup of mead with me while we wait for dinner. I get so few visitors here."

"Brother Tuán, you're so kind, but please don't go to any trouble. Sister Dari and I would be happy just to get out of the rain for the night."

He ignored my protests and continued to pull us up the path past the constant hum of his beehives.

"I've made some new friends since your last visit," he said as we stooped to enter his hut. Indeed, there was a red fox curled up in one corner and a huge badger rooting around under his bed.

He poured us each a generous portion of mead in wooden cups and sat down next to us by the fire. We thanked him and took a long drink as he watched us with pleasure. I have to admit he made the best mead I'd ever tasted.

"Tuán, I don't suppose you know anything about the theft of holy Brigid's bones, do you? They were taken from the church and I've been put in charge of finding them. Do you have any idea who might have taken them?"

I don't know why I was asking a crazy man who lived alone in the woods about the missing bones, but I didn't want to leave any stone unturned.

He hummed a little tune as he stared at the ceiling. I thought he hadn't heard me or was lost in a world of his own. Then he started to sing:

> *Bones, bones, beautiful bones.*
> *Where have they gone to?*
> *Will they come home?*
> *The birds, the beasts, the fishes say,*
> *look in the place the nightingales play.*

Dari glanced over at me and rolled her eyes.

"Yes, Tuán, that's all very good, but . . ."

"Deirdre," he interrupted me with a smile, "have I ever told you the story of how I came to Ireland and what happened to me after I arrived?"

"Yes, Tuán, last time I was here and several times at the monastery when—"

"It's really an amazing tale," he continued. Dari looked quite smug as she sipped her mead.

"It all began a thousand years after Noah's flood. There was no one in Ireland back then, not even the síd folk. I came on a ship from Greece with Agnoman son of Starn as our leader along with fifty other men and women. It was such a fertile land—and so new! We could graze our cattle year round and had to drag them from the pastures each night so they wouldn't overeat and explode."

The exploding cattle of Tuán were a favorite joke among the children of the monastery.

"It was a wonderful time with more babies each year than anyone could count. I had three wives myself and at least a dozen sons and daughters. Everything was going so well until the plague arrived. In less than a month everyone was dead. Everyone but me, that is. I went insane being alone—hard to believe, isn't it? I wandered naked through the mountains and wastelands for years living in caves and fleeing packs of savage wolves. My hair grew down to my waist and my nails became like claws. At last I grew old and lay down in my favorite cave to die."

"This is fascinating, Tuán, but you really don't need to—"

He ignored me as he scooped us each a steaming bowl of stew from the pot over the fire. There was no meat in the stew, but it was a delicious mixture of cream, vegetables, and barley. He also took the bread off the fire and tore the small loaf in half for Dari and me. Tuán continued his story for what seemed like hours, telling us how he had been transformed into a mighty stag, how he had watched waves of new settlers arrive, and how he had become a wild boar, a hawk, and finally a salmon that was eaten by the wife of a local king. He claimed he was then reborn to the queen as a human baby and became a great druid who was converted by Patrick when he first arrived in Ireland. It was useless to interrupt him. Giving the lonely old man a chance to tell his story yet again seemed like a small price to pay for a hot meal and a warm bed.

When he had finished his story, Tuán lay down and fell asleep on his bed with a smile on his face. Dari drained the rest of the mead from her cup and tiptoed quietly towards our bed. One by one, all of Tuán's animal friends, even the badger, curled up next to him and watched me as I banked the fire and blew out the single candle before crawling under the covers with Dari.

We walked all the next day and reached Sleaty just as it was getting dark. There wasn't enough light to do any searching that day and the smell of wet, burnt wood from the church was still strong, so we made our camp a little way off in the forest. We made a porridge for supper, then wrapped ourselves in our blankets, thankful that the rain had finally stopped.

I didn't sleep well that night. I had strange dreams of running through a forest covered in snow trying to find a young girl who kept calling out to me.

When I woke up at dawn, Dari was already heating water over the fire.

"I won't asked how you slept, since you spent most of the night tossing and turning. What were you dreaming about, or do I want to know?"

I rubbed my eyes and took the cup of broth she offered me.

"It was strange. I was in the woods trying to find a little girl. It was freezing. I wonder what it means?"

"Obviously Brigid wants us to go to the North Pole."

"Very funny, Dari. I know not every dream means something, but this one was odd."

"Deirdre, the dream just means you're frustrated about not finding the bones yet. It also means you kicked off your blanket in the night and were cold. That's all."

"Maybe. Let's finish up here. I want to start searching the ruins of the church."

We drank our broth, then Dari knelt on the grass. I joined her and sang the morning psalm, then prayed with her for the sisters and brothers back at Kildare and all of those in need. I added a plea to God that he would help us find something that day that would lead us to the bones. When we finished, we walked down to the banks of the Barrow to wash up.

The site of the Sleaty church was much as we had left it. Brother Fiach's cross still stood tall in the clearing like a lonely sentinel guarding the charred pile of wood behind it.

We began by walking slowly in circles around the church searching the ground for clues. Aside from sheep droppings and the remains of a rabbit recently killed by a falcon, there was nothing to be seen. We then began the filthy task of sorting through the burned remains of the church. It took hours. By the middle of the afternoon Dari and I were both covered in soot. We had searched under every scorched plank twice and found nothing. I had somehow thought that the embroidered cloth of Brigid might have survived, but I knew this was foolish. It would have been the first thing to burn.

"Deirdre, I'm sorry, but there's nothing here." Dari had collapsed on the ground at the foot of the cross. "We did our best, but I'm afraid your grandmother was wrong."

I sat down next to her, exhausted, frustrated, and not a little embarrassed about the whole expedition.

"I guess you're right, Dari. I was so sure we'd find something."

I rubbed my dirty hands through my blackened hair feeling as foolish as I ever had in my life.

"Let's go wash up," Dari said. "I brought some lye soap along. We need to try and clean our tunics as well."

We walked back down to the river and stripped off all of our clothes. As we stood in the cold water trying to rub off as much grime as possible, I couldn't help but laugh at seeing Dari naked. Her head, face, arms, and legs were as black as pitch, but her mid-section where her tunic had covered her was white. She looked down and laughed at herself and me as well. After a long scrub, we climbed out and cleaned our clothes as best we could, then hung them to dry on the bushes.

At that moment I heard a twig snap in the trees behind us. I caught Dari's eye and motioned for her to circle to the right while I moved around to the left. Still naked, we made our way silently to either side of where I had heard the noise.

Crouched behind a thicket of elderberry bushes was a teenage boy with a shepherd's staff holding himself very still in hope that we wouldn't see him. I sprang at once, tripped him as he rose, and threw him on the ground beneath me as I straddled his chest. Dari ran up beside me, picked up his dropped staff and stood above him, aiming the staff at his head. He looked so frightened at the sight of two naked women pinning him to the ground that I almost laughed, but I wanted him scared.

"Who are you?" I growled in his face. "And why were you spying on us?"

"I, please, no, I didn't mean anything by it, ma'am, honest. I was just passing by with the sheep and heard noises from the river. I promise I didn't see anything. Not much anyway."

"Shut up, boy, and don't call me ma'am. Do I look old enough to be your grandmother? What do you know about the church fire? Were you here the night it burned? Did you see anything? Did you start the fire?"

"No, I swear! I was at my father's farm that night. I only come around here during the day sometimes to graze the sheep. I don't know anything!"

He seemed like a simple boy who was telling the truth, but I wasn't done with him yet. I pointed back to where Dari and I had been bathing.

"Do you see that bag over there, shepherd? There's a harp in it. I'm a bard of the court of King Dúnlaing and a druid of the highest rank. Do you know what I'll do to you if you're lying?"

The poor kid looked like he was about to cry.

"No, no, please, don't hurt me! Don't curse me or turn me into anything, I beg you! Look, I found something near the church last week. I'll give it to you if you let me go. It's the only valuable thing I got."

He reached down into his pocket and pulled out a gold cross on a fine silver chain. He gave it to me with his hand trembling.

"Where did you find this?" I demanded.

"In the juniper bushes at the far edge of the meadow near the trail. It was just laying there covered in mud. There was no one around. I didn't steal it, I swear."

I got off him and told Dari to give him back his staff.

"Go home, boy, and don't let me ever catch you spying on naked women again."

"Yes ma'am, he sputtered. "I mean, no ma'am. I mean . . ."

"Just get out of here before I turn you into a toad."

He grabbed his staff and ran down the forest path as fast as his legs would take him. As soon as he was gone, Dari started to laugh, but I was too busy looking at the cross. Its arms were thick at the ends and tapered inward to the center, with a golden ring linking them from behind. I took a deep breath.

"Dari, do you know what this is?"

She looked at it, then nodded slowly.

"Yes. Remember where I grew up."

I held the cross up to catch the afternoon sunlight breaking through the trees and smiled. I had seen that same type of cross in silver just a few days earlier hanging around the necks of the abbot's men.

"Dari, we've got him! This must belong to the abbot. It proves the monks of Armagh burned down the church at Sleaty and stole the bones of Brigid."

Chapter Ten

I t proves no such thing, Sister Deirdre."

I was once again standing inside Sister Anna's hut at Kildare. Dari and I had hurried back to the monastery and arrived late in the evening the day after we left Sleaty. I had told the abbess about everything that had happened, including the voice in my dream, and shown her the cross we had found.

"But, Sister Anna, why else would there be a golden cross of Armagh on the ground at Sleaty if the abbot wasn't responsible for the fire? It has to be his. Don't you remember, he wasn't wearing a cross when he was here? He had to have lost it there. And if he was there and burned down the church, he must have stolen the bones as well."

"I can't believe you studied logic during your school days. The cross means the abbot was at Sleaty, but we already knew that. He told us so himself when he was here. Don't *you* remember? He undoubtedly returned on his trip from Cashel by the same road. At some point while he was there he lost the cross. But his presence at Sleaty doesn't mean he set the fire and it certainly doesn't exonerate you."

She crossed the room to stand in front of me.

"Suppose you show that cross to the abbot. Do you think he will tearfully confess to arson? And what would it matter if he did? Even if the abbot is responsible for the fire, he didn't necessarily steal the bones. There's no reason to think the fire and the theft are connected, in spite of what your grandmother says. The bones of Brigid are the only thing that matters now, not the fire at Sleaty. You have wasted almost a week of precious time chasing after dreams when you should have been carrying out the task I assigned you."

"But Sister Anna—"

"Silence! Foolishness I can forgive, but not lying. You deliberately misled me when you said you were traveling west to talk to farmers about the bones. You never intended to question anyone. Do you hold your vow of obedience to your abbess as meaningless? Does your word mean nothing? Do you think you can break the rules of this monastery because you're a member of the nobility?"

I stood in silence with my head hung low.

"You are dismissed, Sister Deirdre. Go, continue your investigation, if you can spare the time from chasing after dreams. I cannot tell you how disappointed I am in you."

I bowed with what little grace I could muster and left her hut. I didn't want to talk with anyone, not even Dari, so I left the monastery and walked to the tree near the stream where I had used to go with Cormac and sat down beneath it in the darkness. For a long time I wept out of shame and frustration. I thought I had done something useful going to Sleaty, but Sister Anna was right. Although the golden cross meant the abbot had been there, it didn't mean he burned down the church. And there was no proof that the church fire and the missing bones were related. What Sister Anna had said about lying to her was true as well. I had been afraid she would disapprove of the journey, so I had deliberately misled her and gotten Dari involved as well. Maybe Sister Anna was right about me. Perhaps I really did think I was above the rules. I had been a wandering bard for so long that I sometimes didn't think about the limitations I had accepted as a nun.

I considered—and not for the first time—whether I should leave the monastery and go back to being a bard. At least I knew it was something I was good at. Bards don't just play music, of course. We compose praise poetry for kings and warriors, memorize endless genealogies, and celebrate the history of our people in song. We're also responsible for chastising the powerful. I once composed a stinging satire against Ailill, King Dúnlaing's younger son, who was cheating his tenant farmers. The satire made him so ashamed he broke out in blemishes all over his face. Oh, how he hated me after that! In a land where a person's honor is everything, a bard wields enormous authority.

I began my training when I was eight years old. My grandfather on my mother's side had been a bard, as had his mother and father, so there was no trouble entering a profession that was, after all, a family tradition. I had already started my studies at the monastery school each morning, so in the afternoon I would walk down the road to the local bardic school to learn the ancient ways of an Irish poet. Our teachers were the greatest bards of Leinster, including the *ollam* or chief bard of King Dúnlaing. There were about a dozen of us ranging from my age to the late teens, all of us from bardic families. I was the youngest in the school, the only Christian, and the only girl, though there had been many female bards in the past. For hours each day the teachers drilled us in tribal history, epic literature, genealogy, religious rituals, place-name lore, legal texts, and many other subjects. We practiced with our harps until our fingers bled. Most of the students couldn't master the necessary skills and were dismissed from the school by the time they began to sprout a beard. Modesty should make me say it was as grueling a path for me as for the others, but it wasn't. I loved it from the first day. I have always had an excellent memory. I only had to hear a story or song once and it was mine forever.

By the time I was eighteen, I was a fully-trained bard with an honor price half that of a king—if someone dared to harm me, the price they would have had to pay as compensation would have left them and their family in ruin. I traveled throughout Leinster and beyond, singing at banquets and reciting poems commissioned by rulers and noblemen. For the longest and most prestigious compositions, I received three milk cows. For shorter poems I might ask for a goat or two hens. Often I would give these away to the monastery when I returned home, since I had all I needed living with my grandmother.

Now, even though I was a nun, I still retained my rank and privileges as a bard. It would be so easy to set aside the drab tunic of the sisters of holy Brigid and get my colorful robes from the chest in my grandmother's house. I could leave all this behind and no one would think any less of me. Some of the people at the monastery, Eithne chief among them, would be glad to see me go. I doubted Sister Anna would shed any tears at my departure. I might disappoint Dari and Father Ailbe if I left, but they would understand. Besides, they would be right down the road. I could visit them any time I wanted. Maybe I could even find a husband, a decent one this time. Maybe even a prince.

Suddenly I heard the snap of a stick and the sound of footsteps coming toward me. I grabbed a rock and held it ready. I must have been getting paranoid.

"I thought I might find you here. This is where you usually hide when you want to be alone."

It was Dari. She must have wondered where I had gone when I didn't come back to the sleeping hut. She sat down beside me.

"I take it Sister Anna wasn't pleased?"

"That's putting it mildly. She's not mad at you though, just me. She says the cross proves nothing and that I wasted precious time on a fool's errand. But I think she was mostly angry that I lied to her. She thinks I'm a failure as a nun and I agree."

We sat quietly for a few minutes. Finally Dari broke the silence.

"Deirdre, why are you a nun?"

"You know why, Dari. I didn't know what else to do after my son died."

"Was that the only reason? I know it was terrible for you, but you had other options. You could have gone anywhere and started a new life. The whole world is open to someone with your background and abilities. But you became a sister of holy Brigid here at Kildare."

"I suppose I became a nun because this place was familiar to me."

"You've never struck me as a person who clings to the familiar, Deirdre. I think there's more to it than that."

"Alright, Dari, why do you think I became a nun?"

I could almost hear her smile in the darkness.

"I think you were looking for God."

"We're all looking for God, Dari. I didn't need to become a sister of Brigid to do that."

"True, but I think you were looking for something more. I think you wanted a life that forced you to be a better person than you think you are. I think you wanted the challenge that comes from poverty, chastity, and obedience. You see being a nun as a kind of spiritual adventure."

"Dari, that is ridiculous. If I wanted an adventure I'd build a little boat and set myself adrift on the sea like those crazy monks in the west. I'm a nun because I need to do something useful with my life while I figure out what to do next. And if you really want to know, a big part of the reason I'm here at Kildare is so that I don't have to deal with men. I'm tired of them."

Dari laughed and put her arm around my shoulder.

"Deirdre, I think you're hopeless romantic at heart. Are you sure you're over Cormac?"

Of course I was over him. Definitely. He was just a happy memory. But then, why did I keep coming back to this tree?

"Yes, Dari. That was years ago. I'm over him."

"Hmm, maybe."

I wrapped my cloak tighter around myself. The wind from the north was picking up.

"I'm getting cold, Dari. Can we go back to the sleeping hut now and talk about my love life some other time?"

"Sure, but I bet you'll dream about a certain young king tonight, riding into the monastery and sweeping you away to live with him."

"Dari, there must be someone else around here who could be my best friend. Why do I put up with you?"

"Because, my dear, you couldn't live without me."

Chapter Eleven

hree days later, Dari and I set off through the broad grasslands south of Kildare on the way to the court of King Dúnlaing. He was not a Christian, but he had always honored Brigid when she was alive and had protected our monastery since her death. When he was a young king, he had granted her the site of Kildare and the surrounding lands at a very modest annual rent even though the nobles of his tribe had objected. I had known him all my life and had sung for him many times in his feasting hall. Once, when he had been drinking most of the night and was quite inebriated, he told me the story of how he had first met Brigid. I later heard a different version of the tale from Brigid herself.

Only a few weeks after Brigid began her work in Leinster, a young warrior from Connacht was visiting the settlement where Dúnlaing held court. He was anxious to impress the local lord, so when he saw a red fox wander into the king's hall he quickly took out his sword and killed it, thinking he was doing the ruler a favor. The people around him shouted in anger and hauled him before the king, who was furious, since the animal was his trained pet. Dúnlaing told him that unless he could find him another fox that could do the same tricks within three days, he would be killed. When Brigid heard about the man, she took pity on him and determined to save his life—and at the same time gain the favor of the king.

Now it happened that Brigid had a talented pet fox of her own. She took him to the trees just outside the king's settlement and ordered him to stay put, then she entered the gates and fell on her knees before Dúnlaing's hut, praying loudly that he would spare the life of the poor, misguided youth. The king heard her wailing and told her to stop making such a racket unless she could produce a fox like the one he had lost. Calling loudly on God to help her, she clapped her hands three times and her fox came running in from the woods. She put him through a series of tricks—rolling over, fetching a stick, running in circles—that so pleased the king he ordered the young man freed. He then asked if there was anything he could do for a woman who was so favored by her god that wild animals obeyed her. She refused with great drama, claiming that her reward lay in heaven. But the king insisted and so it was then that Brigid asked if she might have a small bit of the king's land on which to build her monastery. Dúnlaing immediately granted her request. The king had never learned the truth about the fox, even after fifty years. Brigid had made me swear on her deathbed that he never would.

Dúnlaing wasn't at his estate on the banks of the Liffey, but instead was at the ancient hill fort of Dún Ailinne to the south. Tonight was the feast of Samain and the king wanted to celebrate it among the tombs of his ancestors.

Samain—or Hallowe'en as some Christians call it—is one of the four holiest days of the traditional Irish year, along with Imbolc at the start of February, Beltaine in May, and the great festival of the god Lug at the beginning of August. Imbolc marks the beginning of spring. It was on that day ten years earlier that Brigid had died, and so we honored her on the anniversary of her death with a grand celebration at the monastery. By coincidence or providence, there was an Irish goddess of the same name whose feast had long been celebrated on the same day. This made it an easy transition for our converts to dance around the fire on Imbolc and sing songs about holy Brigid. I admit it was a shameless appropriation of a pagan holiday on our part, but I think our Brigid would have approved. She never made a fuss over the distinctions between Christian and Irish beliefs

Samain, on the other hand, falls at the start of the dark days of winter and is the time when the barrier between the world of mortals and the realm of the spirits is thinnest. On that night, it's all too easy for someone to pass into the Otherworld without even knowing it—and may the gods help you find your way back. I had heard many stories of children disappearing in the woods on that night or errant travelers meeting strange figures dressed in white near the síd mounds. No sane person ventured out of their farmstead on that evening. Even devout Christians would cross themselves and bar the doors of their homes at sunset.

It was traditional for a tribal king to invite his nobility to a grand feast on Samain. This was called the óenach or gathering and was the highlight of the year for the warrior class. Everyone would wear their finest clothing and jewelry to the feast. It was a chance to show off and boast about what a good year it had been, even if it hadn't. Quite a few marriages were arranged at Samain festivals and more than one drunken hero had been killed by an equally inebriated opponent on that day.

Dún Ailinne was the perfect place for Dúnlaing to hold his Samain gathering each year. The fort itself was huge, with a grand feasting hall in the center. The old stories say that it had once been the greatest capital in Leinster, but that was in a time long past. Nowadays it was deserted except for ceremonial occasions. It lay on a low domed hill with a panoramic view of the surrounding countryside. There was an earthen ring around the whole compound with a rampart wide enough to drive a chariot on. Earlier in the day, Dúnlaing's slaves had set up a dozen tables in the hall around an enormous cooking pit. All the nobles had erected their own colorful tents close by. It was an impressive sight, but the immensity of the fort made the temporary settlement seem small and vulnerable.

Dari and I came to the guest tent at the edge of the fort and dropped off our belongings. One of the slaves gave us water to wash and told us the king and nobles were already gathered for the feast. I knew the king's sons would be present and I was determined to use all my power as a bard to discover if they had taken the bones of Brigid.

I unpacked my harp and was heading out of the tent when Dari grabbed my shoulder.

"Deirdre, are you sure I should come with you? I can stay here and meet you afterwards. I'm sure the servants would bring me something to eat."

"No, Dari, I need you there with me."

"But I'm a commoner. I don't belong in there. You know they won't like it."

"The king will welcome whoever I bring. As for his sons and nobles, I'd be quite happy to make them upset. Angry people make mistakes and say things they shouldn't. They might let something slip about the bones."

"So you're using me as bait?"

"Yes, but also as an extra pair of eyes. Besides, I want you to meet the king. He's a gracious man."

We walked through the cold night to the royal feasting hall. I could hear raucous laughter and smell meat cooking inside. With more flourish than was really necessary, I swept past the guards at the door and marched in with Dari close behind me. Everyone grew suddenly quiet. They all knew me since I had sung at the court many times. The king was sitting at the head of the largest table surrounded by his family and favorite warriors. Most of the people just seemed surprised, especially when they saw Dari, but a few scowled when they saw me approach, notably Illann and Ailill, the king's sons. My cousin Roech, who was sitting next to Illann, turned white as a sheet. Ailill jumped up from his seat and started to move towards me with anger and fear in his eyes, but his brother Illann grabbed him and pulled him back down. King Dúnlaing, however, smiled and rose to bid me welcome. The king stood tall in spite of his years and his green eyes were as bright as ever. He made room for me on the bench next to him, mindful as always of the rank and power of a bard.

"Deirdre, what an unexpected surprise. It's so good to see you again. I'm glad you could join us this evening. My chief bard is sick in bed tonight. I see you brought your harp."

"Yes indeed, my king. It would be an honor to play for you. What better place than Dún Ailinne to sing of your glorious deeds and those of your ancestors?""

"Well, my own glory has dimmed somewhat of late, but I still enjoy the songs of a gifted bard, especially one so young and beautiful."

I smiled at his compliment and bowed in gratitude. He was a kind old gentlemen even though it was clear the years were catching up with him.

"My lord, this is my friend, Sister Darerca. I hope she will also be welcome at your feast."

Dúnlaing grasped Dari's right hand in both of his.

"Of course she is. Welcome, Sister Darerca. The nuns of Brigid's monastery hold a place of honor at my table."

"Thank you, my lord," said Dari with only a hint of trembling in her voice.

We all sat down, Dari next to me, as the feast continued. A slave reached into the great bronze cauldron with a flesh hook and pulled out a pork loin that he served us along with two large mugs of beer. I was famished and greedily cut a slice of the steaming meat with my knife. Dari ate more sparingly. I knew she felt out of place. It was selfish of me to put her through this, but I promised myself I would make it up to her later.

Illann and Ailill sat on the far side of the king, though the way the tables were set up I had a good view of both. They seemed to have suddenly lost their appetites and spent most of the next few minutes discreetly but frantically whispering to each other. Illann kept shaking his head at something Ailill was saying.

As I ate, I made small talk with the king and managed to get Dari in on the conversation. While the king regaled her with some long-ago adventure of his, I looked at the nobles around me. All the men had golden torques fastened around their necks, mostly plain but a few twisted in spirals in the old style. They also wore sturdy bronze bracelets on their arms and decorated brooches to hold their woolen cloaks tight against the chill wind that was blowing through the door. The women were elaborately outfitted with gold rings and pins, faience necklaces imported from Egypt, and amber earrings from the Baltic set in finely-worked silver. Several had silk ribbons tied in their hair. In my coarse woolen tunic with a plain wooden cross about my neck, even the slaves were better dressed than me.

When all the guests had finished dinner and the servants had cleared away the dishes, the king nodded to me and I rose with my harp. The room suddenly grew quiet. I plucked a simple tune on the strings and began to sing:

A prince has reached the lands of the dead,
the noble son of Sétnae,
he laid waste to the valleys of the Fomorians,
under the world of men.

It was a song of ancient Leinster in the days when the ancestors of Dúnlaing and all the warriors present—including my ancestors—had killed the wicked, half-human Fomorians and driven them deep into the darkness of the earth.

I sang of our forbearers, the Gáileóin, great spearmen, and how they had sailed to Ireland from Gaul centuries earlier and seized the eastern part of the island all the way to the Boyne River. I continued with verses celebrating shining Móen, fearless Bresal, and matchless Lorcc, all famous warriors, and their victories against the Ulstermen in days of old. We were the mighty people of Leinster, proud and brave, and most of the guests cheered and pounded the tables when I finished my song. The king's sons gave only polite applause.

Dúnlaing took a golden chain from around his own neck and placed it over my wooden cross as payment for a song well sung. I bowed deeply and thanked him, wondering how much barley I could trade for it next market day to help feed the people at the monastery.

It was good to remind the nobles of Leinster of their glorious ancestors and victories in war, for there had been precious little to celebrate in recent years. The battle in which my father fell thirty years earlier, fighting alongside King Dúnlaing at the Boyne River, was just the first of many disastrous encounters of Leinster with the Uí Néill confederation of Ulster. Defeat followed defeat as they sent chariots south to drive us out of our territory. First they seized the fords of the Boyne, then the coastal lands to the east. There was a great battle for the hill of Tara, but Leinster could no longer hold them back and were forced to retreat yet again. Finally, just four years earlier at Druim Derge, we had lost the whole of the midlands to the Uí Néill up to the plains north of the Liffey. Kildare had once been deep inside Leinster territory, but now we were near the frontier.

I sat back down at Dúnlaing's side as the servants poured wine and the guests broke up into small groups to chat. Now seemed like a good time to mention the real reason for my visit.

"My lord, you are generous as always with your table and gifts, but I wonder if I might risk your anger on this special night by asking about a troubling matter?"

Dúnlaing finished off his first cup of wine and called for another.

"Of course, Deirdre, ask anything you want."

"It's about the bones of holy Brigid."

He looked at me curiously. I suppose he had been expecting me to ask for an extension of time to pay the annual tribute the monastery owed. Sister Anna had sent me to him twice in the past few years to make such a request, which he always had granted.

"The bones? What about them?"

"My lord, you must have heard by now that they're missing."

He put down his wine, a look of horror on his face.

"Missing? What do you mean? Are you saying someone has taken them from the church?"

"Yes, my king, I thought you would have known."

"Illann!" He roared for his eldest son, who jumped up from his seat and rushed to his father's side.

"Yes, my lord, how may I serve you?"

"You could start by telling me if you knew that the bones of Brigid had been stolen from Kildare."

"Well, yes, I had heard some report about such a thing, but it seemed like such a small matter to bother you with when you were busy preparing for the Samain feast that we decided—"

"We? Do you mean others knew about this and said nothing?"

"Yes, but the matter didn't seem worthy of your attention at the time so we—"

"Silence!" he demanded with such a voice that the whole company turned and watched him rise from his seat to tower over his son. The look on his face made my blood freeze.

"Do you know who I am?"

Illann started to sputter something but Dúnlaing cut him off.

"I am the rí, the king of this tribe. It is by my words and deeds that the gods judge all of us here. If I neglect my duty, the powers of earth and sky will destroy me and devastate our lands, as well they should. I cannot be king unless I know what is happening around me. I am the one to decide whether or not something is important, not you or your brother or anyone else in this tribe. And I assure you, boy, if the bones of Brigid have been taken from the church at Kildare, it is very important to me."

All the guests, especially Illann, looked as if they wanted to crawl under their tables and hide. Dúnlaing was old, but I was reminded at that moment why this man had ruled our tribe for so long.

The king looked out at the crowd as he spoke to me.

"Deirdre, do you have any idea who took the bones?"

"No, my lord. I had hoped you might be able to help me find the thief. It has been said that some of your nobles might want to see the monastery weakened."

Dúnlaing nodded, then took his sword from its golden sheath and laid it on the table before him as he spoke to the assembled nobles.

"I will only ask this once: Did any of you take the bones of Brigid?"

No one made a sound. No one moved a muscle. Once Dúnlaing's gaze had finished sweeping the crowd, he spoke again.

"If I learn that any of you has taken the bones, I will personally cut his throat with my sword, even if that man is my own son."

The king sat down again and took a long drink of wine. Illann returned to his seat, his head hanging low. Life slowly began to return to the assembled guests as Dúnlaing turned back to me.

"Deirdre, I cannot tell you how much this grieves me. Brigid was the most holy person I have ever met. To think that anyone would touch her bones—"

Tears began to roll down his cheeks. It was no shame among my people for a man to cry.

"My lord, by the grace of God, I will find those bones and return them to their rightful place at Kildare. I will search this whole island if I need to."

Dúnlaing nodded again.

"Ah, Deirdre, you were always a most determined child, as well as most gifted. I have no doubt that you will recover the remains of Brigid. If there is anything I can do to help—anything—you have only to ask."

"Thank you, my lord. I will not hesitate to call on you."

The joy seemed to have gone out of the feast. The king withdrew to his own tent and the rest of the nobles began to follow in turn. Before Illann and Ailill had a chance to escape, I cornered them away from the others.

"Gentlemen, a good Samain to you."

Illann still looked distressed from the tongue-lashing by his father, but he kept his composure. It was Ailill who spoke first.

"What do you want, Deirdre? Why did you have to come here tonight? We didn't take your precious bones. You have no proof."

"My, Ailill, you do seem defensive. I'm so sorry if I've caused you any trouble. What makes you think I suspect that you're the thieves?"

Before he could answer, Illann spoke.

"Deirdre, why are you here?"

"Because I *do* suspect that you're the thieves. Wouldn't you if you were me? You've always resented that the monastery holds such valuable lands in your father's kingdom. You'd love to have it for yourselves. And your friend Roech acted as guilty as sin when I asked him about it a few days ago. You're a reasonable man, Illann. I'll tell you what I'll do. If those bones are back in the church within the next three days, I won't ask any questions. I'll even tell your father you helped me find them."

"We don't have them!" Ailill shouted. "I swear I'll—"

"You'll do what, Ailill?" I interrupted. "Do want me to sing another satire against you?"

Ailill reached for me, but Illann grabbed his arms and held him back.

"Deirdre," Illann said. "You've delivered your message. I think it's best that you leave now."

"Gladly, my lord."

I turned toward the door.

"By the way, Ailill, if you did steal the bones, I hope the spirits are kind to you tonight. You know they always liked Brigid."

"Well, that was fun."

Dari and I were back in our tent on the edge of the fort. Thankfully, we had it to ourselves.

"Dari, I'm sorry. I hope you at least enjoyed talking with the king."

"Yes, but I was scared to death the whole time. Dúnlaing is one of the most powerful men in Ireland while I'm the youngest daughter of a dirt-poor farmer."

"I think he liked you though. He has a weakness for pretty girls."

I walked to the door flap of the tent and looked around. I wanted to make sure no one was nearby.

"So, what did you think of the king's sons?" I asked her.

Dari yawned and stretched her arms.

"I think they're guilty. Of what, I'm not sure."

"But it has to be the bones."

"Maybe. Illann and Ailill were plainly terrified of you, as was Roech. But did you look at the women in that room?"

"Not really. I mean, I saw some of their jewelry."

"I was looking at more than what they were wearing, Deirdre, and I was listening too. I have good ears. They spent the feast talking about how horrible you looked in your ugly robes and wondering why you would invite some trashy peasant into the king's royal hall."

"Oh Dari, they were just talking. I'm sure they didn't mean it."

"Of course they meant it, but that's not the point. What matters is that whatever plot is going on doesn't involve many people."

"How can you tell that?"

"Because wives know everything their husbands are involved in even if the men think they don't. The only women in that hall who were worried were the two wives of the king's sons and that poor woman married to your sleazy cousin Roech. They looked like they were going to faint from the moment we showed up. They were afraid of what you were going to say to Dúnlaing."

I thought about this for a moment.

"If that's true, maybe we could get one of the wives to talk to us."

Dari shook her head.

"They won't, Deirdre. They may not agree with their husbands and they may even hate them, but they know that if their husbands fall, so do they and their families. No mother is going to sacrifice her children's future to help you."

Dari collapsed on the bed and closed her eyes.

"Deirdre, I'm so tired tonight I can't even pray. Can we go to sleep now?"

"Of course. Let's leave early tomorrow. I want to get back to Kildare as soon as we can."

Dari was asleep before I finished speaking. I pulled the blanket over her and tucked it around her shoulders. I placed my harp in its case and walked out of the tent to the top of the ancient earthen walls of Dún Ailinne. The moon was rising and gave the night an eerie glow.

"Powers of the Otherworld," I whispered to the darkness, "if you will hear the prayer of a Christian on this Samain night, please help me find the bones of Brigid."

A cold wind blew against my face and an owl hooted in the distance. For a moment, I thought I saw someone moving in the shadows at the edge of the woods, but I looked again and there was no one there.

Chapter Twelve

W hen we returned to the monastery the next afternoon, I was thrilled to see smoke rising from the
roof of Father Ailbe's hut. He was sitting outside
his door even though the weather had turned cold. I had a
feeling he was waiting for me.

"Abba, you're back!"

Father Ailbe's real name was Albeus, but no one had used
that name since he left his home in Egypt almost sixty years
ago to make his way to our distant island. The Irish shortened
his name to Ailbe, a common name among us. When I was a
little girl still learning to talk, I couldn't say Ailbe, so I called
him Abba. He thought this was wonderful and so I had called
him that ever since.

I rushed to him as he struggled to his feet and gave him a big
hug. I could feel the bones of his back through his cloak and
knew he had lost more weight. He hadn't been eating properly

lately. I led him back into his hut to sit by the warmth and sweet smell of the peat fire.

His hut was small but comfortable, with a bench by the fireplace and a bed in back. An old chest stood at the foot of his bed and a writing table with a lamp sat beneath the window. A simple cross of twisted reeds hung on the wall, a gift from Brigid herself. Next to the cross was a single shelf holding a few mementos from his travels and a small wooden doll. The doll was unlike any other I had ever seen and I remember being fascinated by it when I was a little girl. The wood was hard like oak, but with a strange reddish color. For a long time I thought it was made from alder, which turns from white to blood-red when cut, but when he finally let me hold it I could tell the weight was wrong. The mouth, eyes, and nose were carefully but not skillfully carved, as if a father unused to working wood had made it for his child. The tunic was sewn with great skill, but the material was woven from coarse flax rather than the soft wool normally used for a doll's clothing. The wood also had bite marks on the limbs and head as if from a teething child, as was common enough, but the oddest thing about the doll was its obvious age. The cloth was frail and yellowed and smelled as if it had been made many years ago. Whenever I had asked Father Ailbe about it, he would only say that it had belonged to a patient of his long ago.

I brought him a hot cup of broth from the small pot over the hearth and sat next to him to make sure he drank it.

"Thank you, my dear. That does taste good."

Some of the broth was stuck to his white beard, so I took a cloth and wiped it away. He winced.

"You don't need to fuss about me so, Deirdre. I'm not an invalid yet. And in any case, I hear you have a great deal more to worry about than an old man with a messy face. I stopped by your grandmother's house on the way here. She told me all the latest news, including your trip back to Sleaty and the discovery of the Armagh cross."

I had gone to my grandmother's house the day after my dressing down by Sister Anna. Over a slice of warm bread with lots of butter, she urged me to pay no attention to the disbelief of the abbess, though she said I should have told Sister Anna the truth about where I was going. She believed the cross was an important clue in my search, though I wasn't so sure.

"Yes, Sister Anna has put me in charge of finding the bones of Brigid," I said to Father Ailbe. "But it's been over two weeks since we discovered they were missing and I'm no closer to solving the mystery. Oh, Abba, what am I going to do?"

He stood and put his medical bag on his shoulder.

"Why don't you come with me on my rounds?" he said. "There are a couple of patients I need to check on. We can talk on the way."

Father Ailbe had been born into a wealthy merchant family in the coastal metropolis of Alexandria. His family lived next to the old Jewish Quarter of the city. He grew up speaking Greek, but he was also fluent in Latin, Coptic, Aramaic, and several other languages. He had studied with the greatest scholars of his day, mostly at the fabled Library of Alexandria. The library had once held tens of thousands of papyrus scrolls, but in Father Ailbe's youth Christian fanatics had burned almost all of them, believing they were tools of the devil. The remaining academics at the library spent their time teaching young people like Father Ailbe and frantically copying texts in hope that some might survive. But every few years the Parabolans, as the Christian brotherhood called themselves, would rouse themselves into a fury and destroy any books they could find. By the time Father Ailbe had reached his late teens, the collection had been sadly depleted.

One day the Parabolans came to the library with torches in hand to destroy the building and its contents once and for all. The head librarian quickly gathered a few precious scrolls and hid them in a small wooden chest. Father Ailbe was studying there that day and was a favorite student of the head librarian, so he was given the chest. He told the young man to keep them safe for the future, then sent him out the back door while he and the other librarians held off the mob in the front at the cost of their own lives. Father Ailbe took the chest home and protected it, as he had promised, reading the scrolls at night with the curtains drawn. It contained lost treatises of Aristotle, the complete works of Sappho of Lesbos, gospels ascribed to Peter and Judas, and other priceless works unknown elsewhere in the Roman world. When Father Ailbe came to Ireland, he brought the chest with him for fear it would be discovered and destroyed in Egypt. Now it sat at the foot of his bed, holding the last remnants of the great Library of Alexandria. I had spent countless hours over the years in his hut reading these scrolls by candlelight.

By his own admission, Father Ailbe was an impious youth. Although he was a gifted student and a passionate learner, he and his friends spent much of their free time roaming the back alleys of Alexandria picking fights and seducing girls. Over the objections of his father, he chose medicine over commerce, though he continued to travel frequently on trade missions for his family. He had often told me of his journeys to Constantinople, Jerusalem, and even India. But one night in his early twenties, he witnessed something that changed his life forever.

The pagan philosopher and mathematician Hypatia, a woman of extraordinary intelligence who attracted many Christian students to her school in Alexandria, had been murdered some years before Father Ailbe was born. The local bishop Cyril, later declared a saint, was jealous of her success and had ordered the Parabolans to hunt her down as a witch. Few pagans dared to raise their heads in Alexandria after her death, but one disciple of Hypatia named Sophia quietly continued her work in mathematics and philosophy. She was a teacher and dear friend of Father Ailbe and lived near his family.

It was many years before Father Ailbe would tell me the whole story, but one night the Parabolans found Sophia and dragged her into the street. By the light of the full moon, they tore her apart like wolves. Father Ailbe had been away tending to a patient, but he found her remains when he returned home that morning. He gathered up the tattered pieces of her body and buried them himself in his family's tomb. Unable to understand how men who claimed to follow Christ could do such a thing, he decided to devote his life to the true service of God. Although raised a Christian, he had never cared much for religion before that terrible night. Now, over the fierce protests of his family, he turned his back on the world, left the chest with the precious scrolls to a trusted friend, and became a monk of holy Anthony at a desert monastery east of the Nile.

He would never tell me exactly why, but a few years later he left the monastery, retrieved the chest, and sailed away from Alexandria on a grain ship bound for Rome where he stayed with family friends. While there, he became acquainted with Pope Leo and treated his malaria. Leo had several Irish slaves in his household and so Father Ailbe, curious about this distant land, spent time with them tending to their illnesses and learning their language. A few months later he received the Pope's blessing to go to Ireland as a missionary. He travelled north to Milan, then across the Alps and Gaul to the channel where he took the only boat he could find to Britain, even though it was a broken down wreck with a drunken captain. At last he made his way to the western coast of Britain and sailed from there with some wine merchants to Munster. He so impressed the king at Cashel with his medical skills that he was allowed to start a church at nearby Emly, where he worked among the local tribes for many years. When Bishop Conláed died, Brigid asked Father Ailbe to come to Kildare to take his place. He had always admired our founder, so he left one of the priests he had trained in charge in Emly and came to our monastery as our new bishop.

"So, what are you going to do about the bones?" pondered Father Ailbe as we walked along. "Why don't you tell me first how things went with Dúnlaing."

I told him.

"Yes, that's what I would expect the king to do. He always held Brigid in high regard and would never suffer one of his people to touch her remains. But you were right to begin your search with him. If nothing else, you've caused a stir among the nobility of his court. Word will spread across Leinster about the bones and someone who knows something might tell Dúnlaing, then he can tell you."

"Abba, do you think the king would really kill one of his own sons if he turned out to be the thief?"

"Oh yes. No king could allow a challenge to his authority like that. I don't think he's ever liked Illann anyway. The boy doesn't have the qualities to make a good ruler. Too devious, too much living in the shadows. And his brother Ailill is nothing but a bully."

We came to the hut of his first patient, an old man whose leg had been injured weeks earlier when a tree he was chopping down fell on top of him. He had begged the man to let him amputate it, but he wouldn't listen. Now it was swollen and oozing a greenish pus that smelled so foul I almost fainted. Father Ailbe gave him something for the pain, but he shook his head as we left and said the man wouldn't last another week.

People always said Kildare was the best place in Ireland to be sick. Father Ailbe had received his medical education in Alexandria under the leading physicians of the day. In the years since, he had moved far beyond the theories of Hippocrates and Galen into practical medicine based on observation and an open mind. He was a master of herb lore as well as surgery. I had seen him cut into a young woman after a long and fruitless labor to remove twin girls from her womb. With any other physician, this would have been a death sentence for the mother, but with his skillful technique and strict attention to cleanliness, the woman returned to good health to raise her daughters.

"What about the abbot of Armagh?" I asked as we left the farm. "That man is as slippery as an eel. Sister Anna agrees that he might have stolen the bones or is at least taking advantage of the theft."

Father Ailbe nodded.

"I wouldn't put anything past the abbot. I met him when he was a boy at Armagh. Even then he was plotting and scheming. I can tell you Patrick never liked him. My old friend would be appalled that such a man is now in charge of the church there."

"But I hate to believe that any Christian, even the abbot, would steal the bones of Brigid."

"Deirdre, my child, I'm afraid that churchmen can be as deceitful and avaricious as anyone else in this world. I'm sorry to say that such thefts are not unknown among Christians in the Mediterranean world. Once, when I was in Jerusalem, I saw monks from different factions at the Church of the Holy Sepulcher come to blows over a missing baby tooth supposedly belonging to our Lord. It turns out a visiting bishop from Antioch had snuck into the church one night and taken the tooth back to Syria. They were still fighting over possession of the tiny relic last I heard."

"What about Cormac? Do you think he could have taken the bones?"

I pulled Cormac's letter out of my satchel and handed it to him. He read it quickly as we walked.

"I think our young prince paid too much for the Alexander coin, but the letter is intriguing. It could be he has some evidence that implicates someone or he may be trying to lead you astray. With Cormac you never really know. He was my best student—aside from you of course—but after all those years I never felt as if I understood him."

"I'm going to his inauguration in Glendalough soon," I said. "I'll question him then."

"Really? It will be interesting to hear what he has to tell you." He looked at me in a knowing way.

"Are you sure you're ready to see him again, my dear?"

"Abba," I said, embarrassed in spite of myself, "that was over years ago."

"Deirdre, if there's anything I've learned during my life, it's that love can endure for a very long time."

We walked to a small farm east of Kildare where a three-year old girl named Caitlin lay dying. I had known her parents for years. They were tenant farmers of the monastery who lived with their five children. The mother and father were poor, but they were hard workers who made sure there was always enough food on the table.

"How is our little one doing today?" asked Father Ailbe when he saw the mother outside the hut. The rest of the family was working in the fields.

"Oh, Father, it's so good to have you back." She gave us both a hug and led us inside. "My little Caitlin—"

She began to cry.

"I'm sorry," she said. "It's just so hard to see her this way. She was always the most lively of my children, running all over the farm and getting into everything. Now she can barely walk across the hut. She drinks well enough, but she's not eating as much as she should. I make special broths for her, rich with fat and honey, but she never finishes a bowl."

Father Ailbe went to the bed where Caitlin was sleeping. She looked pale and worn. He sat down beside her and took her hand as he felt her pulse, then pulled back the blanket to listen to her heart. She woke up and smiled when she saw him. She had the most beautiful eyes I had ever seen.

"Abba?" She had heard me call him by that name on an earlier visit. He smiled and stroked her cheek

"Yes, my darling, it's me. I couldn't stay away from you long. How do you feel?"

"Sleepy." She yawned and stretched her arms. They were so thin.

"Rest then, little one. And dream sweet dreams."

He covered her up and tucked the blanket around her, then kissed her on the forehead. She smiled again and drifted back to sleep. Her mother followed us outside, where she and Father Ailbe sat on the bench by the door.

"Father, is there anything you can do for my little girl?"

Father Ailbe took her hand. I saw that there were tears in his eyes.

"I'm so sorry. I've seen many of these cases over the years and they always have the same ending. The best I can do for Caitlin is keep her comfortable and remember her in my prayers. I'll leave more medicine for her in case the pain returns. I'll check on her again in a few days."

He held the mother in his arms for a long time as she sobbed. Finally, she wiped her eyes and said she had better go and check on Caitlin. I hugged her and told her I would be back to visit as soon as I could. Father Ailbe and I walked away in silence. The death of children always affected him the most. I put my arm around him and wished there was something more I could do.

We reached the monastery gate and Father Ailbe turned toward his hut while I went to the kitchen to help with the evening meal. But before he left, I had to ask him.

"Abba, do you think I can find the bones in time?"

He smiled at me the same way he did when I was a student and had grown frustrated at some difficult school lesson.

"You know, when I was in India long ago, I came one day to the cave of a holy man I had been seeking because he had a great reputation as a seer, much like your grandmother. He was a Buddhist monk who lived next to a river high in the mountains beneath a crystal blue sky. Before he would even talk to me, he made me take off all my clothes and sit silently with him for three days watching the waters flow past. Then at last I asked him if I would ever find what I was searching for in life, my true path, my calling. He shrugged and said he didn't know because the future hadn't happened yet. Then he went inside his cave and fell asleep."

"Is that little tale supposed to encourage me?"

He smiled again. "Maybe not, but I think he was trying to tell me that there's always hope."

Chapter Thirteen

On a clear day you can see the Wicklow Mountains from Kildare, but on the morning Dari and I started our journey to the high valley of Glendalough it was raining with a cold fog hugging the fields and forests around the monastery. We walked east all morning to the Liffey River, then followed the south bank as it rose into the foothills. We stopped for a late lunch under an ancient dolmen tomb made from a large slab of stone placed like a tabletop on three smaller, vertical slabs. It was a tight squeeze, but I was so tired of being wet I was grateful just to be out of the rain. Some people said such enclosures were lucky places for a woman to take a man if she wanted to become pregnant, but soaked as I was, sex was the last thing on my mind.

I remembered a story people told of Brigid when she was caught out in the rain one day. She had been herding sheep a few miles from the monastery when an afternoon storm came up quickly and soaked her to the skin. She was near an old stone shed, so she went inside to take off her wet cloak. Just as she approached the door, the sun burst through the clouds and started to shine brightly. She was blinded by the sudden change in light and stumbled into the shed. She saw what she thought was a white rope stretched across the room and hung her cloak on it to dry. But it was in fact a narrow beam of light shining into the dusty room from a small hole in the wall. When some shepherds came by a few minutes later and saw this, they fell on their knees and praised God. I asked Brigid about this story once. She smiled and said people are always looking for miracles. If they wanted to believe she had hung her cloak on a sunbeam, who was she to say they were wrong?

Dari and I spent the night at an abandoned church and arrived at Glendalough late the next afternoon. Cormac's small kingdom was centered on the two lakes that gave the valley its name—*Glen da lough*—"glen of the two lakes." The lower lake was the smaller of the two, while the upper lake just to the west lay beneath two steep, rounded hills covered with oak and pine. It was one of the prettiest places in Ireland and I regretted that we didn't have more time to enjoy it. Cormac's settlement was on the eastern shore of the lower lake and it was there all the festivities were to take place. There were tents for guests set up near the royal feasting hall and a large field had been prepared by the lake for purposes unknown.

The activities were already underway when Dari and I walked into the crowd. It was a mixed group of nobles and commoners, so I hoped Dari wouldn't feel out of place. At last I saw Cormac in the middle of a crowd of warriors.

He looked very much as he had when I had last seen him a few years earlier. He was still as handsome and radiant as ever, with curly blond hair and broad shoulders. He was of average height, but somehow had always seemed larger than life.

I had to remind myself to breathe as he spotted me and smiled. He excused himself from his companions and walked over to give me a strong embrace. His touch brought back so many memories.

"Deirdre, how are you? Is that what they're making nuns wear these days? Please make yourself at home in my guest house, not in one of these tents. I'll have my slaves bring you a change of clothing."

"Thank you, no, Cormac," I managed to sputter. "I'll gladly stay in your guesthouse, but I'm afraid these robes come with living at the monastery. I think they were designed to discourage the interest of men."

He laughed and kissed my hand. "Not even those clothes could hide beauty such as yours."

I blushed like a schoolgirl. I didn't dare look at Dari.

"I've missed you, Deirdre, but I'm so glad you could come today. I've got a great surprise in store for everyone."

He turned and smiled at Dari.

"I can't believe I have the honor of hosting two sisters of Brigid today."

"Cormac, this is my friend Dari. She's here to make sure you don't try to seduce me."

Now Dari blushed. Cormac laughed again.

"Welcome, Sister Dari. I can't make you any promises about Deirdre, but at least I'll try to be discreet."

Cormac clapped his hands and a servant appeared.

"Move the belongings of these two sisters into my guest house and give them the finest room. Make sure there's a flask of wine there for them, the good vintage."

The slave bowed silently.

"You're going to spoil us, Cormac."

"I hope so. I want you to make a good report of me to Sister Anna."

He turned to Dari.

"My dear, would you like to go to the guest house and freshen up before the ceremony begins? I'll take good care of Deirdre while you're gone."

"Thank you, my lord. I would like to splash some water on my face and give you two a chance to catch up."

She gave me a quick look that I recognized as a note of caution, then followed the slave. When she was gone, Cormac suddenly looked serious.

"I never had a chance to tell you, Deirdre, but I'm so sorry about your son."

"Thank you, Cormac. It was a—difficult time."

He hugged me again, then held my hand as we walked.

"How is Father Ailbe?"

"He's doing well. I know he misses you. You should come to Kildare for a visit."

"I promise I will, as soon as I get settled in as king. I'd love to see everyone again."

"Will you have some time to meet with me tomorrow? I know you're busy now, but I believe we have something to talk about."

"Yes, tomorrow would be good. I have some information which I think will surprise you."

"What kind of information?"

"You'll see then. Forgive me, but I've got to see to some last minute details. I'll have one of my girls take care of you. Eat something, please. You're looking skinny, you know."

He called for one of his slaves, an older woman, who showed me to the guest quarters. It was only fair that I waited until tomorrow to speak with him about the bones. Today rightfully belonged to him.

"So, what do you think of Cormac?" I asked Dari.

She was trying on one of the colorful cloaks hanging in our room.

"He's a hard man to read, but he definitely wants something from you. Besides your body, that is," she added.

"I think he would be disappointed with my body, Dari," I sighed. "I'm not sixteen anymore, I've got stretch marks from giving birth, and in spite of what everyone keeps telling me, I know I've put on weight."

"Don't sell yourself short, Deirdre. You're a beautiful woman. Cormac knows you're not a teenager. But when a man reaches thirty, unless he's a fool, he wants a woman who has more to offer than just beauty."

"I don't have anything to offer him, Dari. I'm a nun, remember?"

"Yes, but you're still in love with him."

"I am not! That was a long time ago and it's over."

"I saw the way you looked at him."

"Dari, I brought you along to watch him, not me."

"Actually, I think Sister Anna sent me, to keep you out of his bed."

"I'm not getting into his bed! I'm a nun!"

Just then the old slave woman knocked on the door and entered.

"My ladies, the ceremony is about to begin."

I had never doubted that Cormac would be a king some day even though a son did not automatically succeed his father. The nobles of a tribe could choose one of their own to take the crown if they thought a king's son unfit to rule. Any prince who was crippled or disfigured would of course not be eligible to be king since a ruler must be free from blemish, but a son could also be passed over if the warriors felt he lacked the ability to rule a tribe and lead an army in war.

A new king was chosen by the *tarbfess* or "bull sleep." In this ritual, a special bull was sacrificed and cooked. A respected man of the tribe was then chosen to eat some of the meat and drink the broth with druids chanting over him while he fell asleep. When he woke, he told everyone who he had seen in his dreams. If the nobles approved, that man would become king. I suspected that Cormac had arranged for one of his most loyal supporters to be the guest of honor at the recent bull feast of his tribe. My old friend never took chances.

Like most kings who assume their thrones at a young age, Cormac was eager to establish his legitimacy. When we came out of the guesthouse and made our way to the field surrounded with blazing torches, I at last realized what he was about to do. He had chosen to perform an ancient ceremony of inauguration, the origins of which stretched back to the beginnings of our people, though it had not been done for many years. All the members of his tribe had gathered that chilly evening to watch, along with visiting guests. He had instructed one of his men to make sure Dari and I had a particularly good view.

His servants led a beautiful white mare into the field and paraded it three times around the assembled crowd. Knowing what was about to happen, his warriors began shouting obscene comments at Cormac. Dressed in his finest clothes, he stood grinning in the middle of the large open circle on top of a short wooden platform. The groomsmen brought the horse close to Cormac, though facing away from him. With great ceremony, he removed his clothes until he stood naked before us with only a golden torque about his neck. His eyes finding me in the front row of the crowd, he smiled and winked. Then he turned to the mare and lifted her tail with his hand.

I had heard my grandmother speak of the horse ceremony before, not hiding her disgust in spite of her love of tradition. I never imagined that any king would actually perform it in my lifetime, especially with me only a few feet away. She had said the horse represented the sovereignty of the land and that for a king to possess it was to become master of the fertile fields, rivers, and mountains of his kingdom. I understood the symbolism of the rite, but it didn't make it any easier to watch. I thought Dari was going to faint. She turned to leave, but I held her firmly in place. Her face was a mixture of horror and disgust as the ceremony continued.

Cormac had somehow aroused himself enough to penetrate the mare while several of his men held the surprised beast still. After what seemed like hours, but was a few minutes at most, Cormac let out a loud groan and withdrew. The crowd erupted in cheers as he turned, still naked, to wave at them. The grooms then led the horse away while the king stepped down off the platform and walked to the edge of the field where an enormous iron cauldron filled with water had been readied over a roaring fire. At first, I thought Cormac was going to boil himself alive, but then I remembered the second part of the ceremony.

The mare was brought to the cauldron where Cormac stroked her forehead and spoke to her gently. He then took an axe from one of his warriors and brought it down on the animal's neck, killing the creature with one blow. His attendants swiftly butchered the horse into small pieces and threw the bloody chunks into the boiling pot. As Cormac stood shivering and chatting with his warriors, the mare was turned into a stew.

After a time, the fire was extinguished so that the broth could cool. A little while after that, Cormac climbed still naked into the steaming cauldron and stood with his arms raised to the sky. After a druid chanted some prayers, the king dipped his hands into the broth and brought it to his mouth to drink. His warriors blew long, curved horns and more cheers followed as Cormac shouted that he and the horse were now one. He grabbed a large piece of meat floating on top and began to eat, then invited his people to come forward and join with him in the feast. All the members of his tribe then filed past the cauldron, along with the assembled guests, and dipped in their bowls as musicians played and the rest of the banquet food was brought out onto tables that had suddenly appeared. It was a grand occasion, but I had lost my appetite and politely declined a cup of broth.

On the way back to the guest house, Dari looked as disturbed as I had ever seen her.

"Deirdre, that was without a doubt the most sickening, degrading thing I have ever seen. Why didn't you let me leave?"

"Because it would have been a terrible insult to Cormac. I'm sorry, but you can't just walk out of a ceremony like that."

"Well, I swear by holy Jesus himself that you're not going to drag me to one of these so-called noble rituals again. The poor horse!"

"Look, Dari, I—"

Suddenly I whipped around and looked behind me. One of Cormac's warriors, a tall, dark-haired man with a jagged scar down his right cheek, had just passed by us. He had nodded to us in a pleasant way and continued on toward Cormac's feasting hall, undoubtedly for a raucous night of drinking and celebration with his new king. It had taken me a moment to realize what he was wearing. His tartan cloak was dark green with a distinctive black and gold pattern throughout, just like the cloth left behind at Tamun's farm. Then I saw on the back where the cloak met his thighs that a piece was missing.

Chapter Fourteen

T he next morning Cormac sent word that he would receive me in his feasting hall. It was nothing more than a larger version of a typical village hut, circular with mud walls and a high thatched roof. The dark interior, with benches all around and a blazing fire in the center, smelled of boiled meat and the sweat of men. Cormac was sitting alone in the room on a chair at the front of the hall, scratching the chin of an enormous wolfhound at his feet.

"Please forgive the informal setting for our meeting, Deirdre, but I'm weary of ceremony after yesterday's strenuous activities." He then called a slave to bring me a cup of wine, which I accepted.

"I hope you don't mind if Muirne here keeps us company while we talk. She just weaned a litter of puppies and could use a bit of rest. Tell me how you liked the horse sacrifice. Wasn't it spectacular? Nobody has done anything like that since Niall of the Nine Hostages became high king."

"You seemed to have enjoyed it more than the horse."

Cormac burst into laughter. "You're probably right. But still, you didn't come here to discuss such crude matters. We need to talk about the bones of Brigid."

I was so furious at Cormac I thought I might throttle him then and there. I knew one of Cormac's own warriors had been hiding near Kildare on Michaelmas. I had thought the king's sons were guilty of stealing the bones, but now I wondered. I had brought the piece of tartan cloth along to reveal at the right moment.

"Yes, Cormac. As you know, the bones draw many pilgrims to Kildare who come in search of hope and healing."

"Not to mention increasing the power and income of the monastery, especially at the expense of the churchmen of Armagh," he interjected. Cormac cared little for Christianity or any other religion, but he knew ecclesiastical politics.

"I won't deny that the theft of the bones threatens the existence of our monastery. You know how precarious our situation is. The authorities in Armagh, not to mention some in Rome, would love to shut us down. A thriving religious community run by women is the last thing they want. Without the bones of Brigid, visitors will stop coming to Kildare, donations will cease, and we won't be able to continue our ministry to the poor."

I thought I'd try playing on his sense of guilt. He'd been a student at Kildare, he respected Sister Anna, and had been like a son to Father Ailbe.

"Cormac, if I can't find those bones soon, the wolves from Armagh will move in for the kill. The abbot will call a synod of bishops and have us placed under their jurisdiction. Sister Anna will be removed and the sisters will be put to work washing their clothes and cooking their meals. Everything depends on finding those bones."

He pushed the wolfhound away with his foot and poured me another glass of wine.

"You don't think I stole them, do you, Deirdre?" His face was a mask of innocence.

"I think you would do almost anything to increase your power. If possessing those bones would somehow help you, then yes, I think you might have done it."

He smiled and drank his wine in one gulp before calling for another flask. I had seen him drink men under the table at feasts without showing the slightest sign of fading.

"I'm honored you think me so devious. I confess that as soon as I heard the news, I almost wished I had stolen them. Moving the shrine of Brigid to our valley would be a coup for me. All the pilgrims who used to go to Kildare would find their way here instead. You know I don't believe in the Christian god, but I am intrigued by the potential of Christianity. Even though I'm still not convinced much will come of your faith in Ireland, I do like to hedge my bets. We get a fair number of religious visitors even now worshipping at the well of Moccu near the upper lake. He was a holy man, a druid, you know, in my great-grandfather's day, who could supposedly heal the sick. He was terribly afraid of fire for some reason and asked that his bones be placed in the well so that they would always be surrounded by water. People do have strange notions. But the peasants who visit the well report that the water flowing over his remains is good for healing, especially eye diseases."

I had once visited Moccu's well with my grandmother, who had never been able to see anything clearly at a distance. After dunking her head in the freezing water all morning, the only thing she had to show for it was very wet hair. I think she would have thrown the old druid's bones to the dogs if she could have torn away the heavy slab covering the mouth of the well.

Cormac continued. "Yes, a church with the bones of Brigid would make a fine addition to the shrines of my little valley. Visitors would come here from all over Leinster and beyond. And if the remains of Brigid didn't work for them, ailing pilgrims could walk to the far side of the lake and give Moccu a try."

So that was it. He wanted to use the bones of Brigid to make Glendalough a pilgrim destination, pagan or Christian, take your pick.

"You seem to have considered this carefully, Cormac."

"Oh, I'm just thinking out loud. You realize, of course, it wouldn't do me much good to have the bones here without a good Christian to oversee the shrine. And I don't mean some bumbling fool of a monk. I would need someone of real intelligence who knows how to run things properly and get results. Someone respected by the common people. A Christian, of course, but one who doesn't shun the old ways when there's a tidy profit to be made. And since Brigid is of particular interest to women, I would need a woman to manage my new church."

It took me a moment to realize what he was suggesting. I was on my feet.

"You can't be serious, Cormac. You think I would leave the monastery at Kildare and come into these mountains to serve you? You think I would betray Sister Anna and Father Ailbe to be your token Christian?"

I took the piece of tartan cloth out of my pocket and slammed it on the table in front of him.

"How do you explain this?"

Cormac took the cloth and looked at it, turning it over in his hands.

"Tamun chased away one of your men hiding in his bushes on Michaelmas and he lost this on a hawthorn tree. I saw the very man last night here with his torn cloak. Now, do you want to give me the bones now or do I bring Sister Anna here? She would eat you alive."

"It belongs," he said, "to Techmar, one of my best warriors. His farm is on the borderlands near Dúnlaing's territory. He told me some crazy old farmer near the monastery had chased him away. I thought it might be Tamun. He once took after me with pitchfork when I tried to steal some eggs from his chickens."

"Well, I'm glad you at least admit to stealing the bones."

"I'm not admitting anything."

"Cormac, I swear, if you don't give me those bones I will call on God himself to strike you down! I will compose a satire so fierce you will die of shame! I will get my grandmother to curse you with such impotence that you'll never come near a woman or horse again! I will—"

Cormac raised his hand.

"Deirdre, before you continue, I have something to show you."

He pulled a small piece of parchment from under his cloak and handed it to me. It was folded and bore a broken seal. I pushed the two outer flaps of the letter together and saw the seal:

It was a Chi-Rho, a first two letters of the name of Christ in Greek, an ancient sign used by a few bishops and monasteries, but in Ireland only by the churchmen of Armagh.

"Where did you get this, Cormac? Why are you showing it to me? If you're trying to shift the blame—"

"Deirdre, Techmar and some of my border guards came across a stranger passing through the northern edge of our lands by night several weeks ago. They killed him and found this on him. Please open it."

I opened the letter and saw the writing was in Ogam letters. It had no salutation or closing signature, only three words:

||||......||||.//////..... /.....||||.....||/.|||| ||..//////||||.|||||

"My God, Cormac."

"So you can read it?"

"Of course I can read it. I'm a druid, remember?"

"Yes, I know. The sender was really quite clever. Only druids and royalty know Ogam. I'm sure the messenger didn't know what it said nor would almost anyone else who found it."

"Are you sure this is genuine?"

"Positive. Techmar found it in the stranger's satchel and brought it to me that same night. I trust him completely. I broke the seal and read it."

I looked at the words again: *Kildare—Michaelmas—Lorcan.*

"Why didn't you send word to us? Give us some kind of warning? You saw Lorcan's name!"

Lorcan was a notorious outlaw who lived on Lambay Island just off the eastern coast. He was a cruel and murderous man who controlled all the pirates, brigands, and thieves in Ireland.

"I didn't tell you because I wanted to find out what was going on first. Don't worry, I didn't leave you unprotected. I sent a dozen of my best warriors to watch in the woods around the monastery on Michaelmas. That's why Techmar was hiding in Tamun's bushes. As it turned out, nothing happened."

"Where did this messenger your men killed come from? Where was he heading?"

"From what I can tell, he must have come south from Armagh through the forests along the coast before he turned west into the mountains. He was taking the long way around, skirting Dúnlaing's lands. He didn't want the king to find him. Care to guess whose farm he was on the path to?"

There was only one farmstead on the border between the small kingdom of Glendalough and Dúnlaing's realm.

"Illann, the king's son."

"Yes."

"Cormac, the abbot comes from an Uí Néill royal family. He would know how to write Ogam letters. He's probably the only one at Armagh that does. And Illann certainly could read them. Do you realize what this means?"

"Yes, it means Illann and Ailill are working with the abbot of Armagh to bring down the monastery at Kildare. It wasn't just the king's sons who were behind the theft of the bones, it was the abbot too."

I had to have another cup of wine.

"Cormac, this was on the latch of the empty chest that held Brigid's bones." I handed him the silk ribbon from my pocket.

"I thought it must have been a member of the nobility who stole the bones, but pirates would have plenty of these, wouldn't they?"

He took the ribbon.

"Very high quality. You don't see many like this anymore. But yes, Lorcan probably has more Byzantine silk than all the kings of Ireland."

"Cormac, may I keep the letter?"

"Of course. It could be useful to you."

I folded it and placed the letter inside my cloak pocket along with the ribbon.

"No wonder Illann and Ailill looked like they were going to soil themselves when I showed up at the Samain feast. They must have thought I knew something and was going to expose them that night."

"Yes, I heard about what happened."

"Cormac, could the thief have slipped past your guards at Kildare that night?"

"It is possible," he said. "Professional thieves are very good at their job. We couldn't risk putting a man inside the monastery to guard the church itself. Sister Anna, bless her heart, doesn't completely trust me. She might have thought I wanted to steal the bones myself."

"But even if the bones weren't stolen on Michaelmas," I said, "we know the abbot and Dúnlaing's sons hired Lorcan to take them. I should go to the king. He'll deal with his sons and ransom the bones of Brigid, which must be on Lorcan's island."

Cormac shook his head.

"Deirdre, think for a moment. The only proof you have of a conspiracy is a piece of parchment with a broken seal and a few Ogam words on it. And remember, the message never got through to Illann and Ailill. The bones are missing, so they must have arranged the theft somehow, but we don't have proof. The letter is certainly incriminating, but it's not enough. Illann will claim I made the seal and forged the letter. The abbot will back him up. They'll say I'm just trying to sow discord in Dúnlaing's kingdom so I can expand my own power. Remember, Dúnlaing is old, but he's no fool. He doesn't trust me."

"I'm not sure I trust you either, Cormac," I said. "*Did* you forge the letter?"

"If I took an oath that I didn't, would you believe me?"

"Maybe."

He stood up from his chair and looked me straight in the eye.

"Deirdre, daughter of Sualdam, I am Cormac, son of Domnall, king of the tribesmen of the glen of the two lakes. I swear by the god by whom my tribe swears, this letter is genuine."

Cormac was the most cunning man I had ever met, but he knew that a tribe depended on the power of its king to speak the truth. A ruler who swore falsely would bring down disaster on his people, if not by the will of the gods, then by the very fabric that held the universe together. He might not believe in much, but Cormac was a man of honor in this respect.

"I believe you, Cormac. I'm sorry I doubted you."

He sat back down.

"Don't be. If I were in your place, I would doubt me too."

"But what should I do now? If I can't go to Dúnlaing with this letter, then I need to find better proof. Should I go to Lorcan's island?"

"No! He would kill you the moment you set foot there. I've already started to make inquiries among some men who have contacts with Lorcan. It may take time, but I'll find out if he has the bones."

"I don't have much time, Cormac."

"Then look for other kinds of proof. We know now that Dúnlaing's sons are working with Armagh. You'll never pin anything on the abbot, he's too clever, but the king's sons might make mistakes, especially Ailill. You've got my eyes and ears working for you too. And please, Deirdre, be careful."

Cormac stood up and walked around the table to sit beside me, stepping over the dog.

"You know, I meant everything I said before. Whether you find the bones or not, it would be wonderful to have you here in my valley. I still think about the nights together when we were in school. I was a fool to ever let you go. You're smart and courageous and, like I said yesterday, quite beautiful. I wasn't proposing you come here to live alone in some dark church. I would like you to be my wife."

I was so taken back by his words that all I could do was stare at him.

"I'm serious, Deirdre. And I don't mean just to share my bed, but to work with me as a trusted advisor. I would marry you *lánamnas comthinchuir*—the highest form of marriage with full rights and joint authority. You would be entitled to half my goods and property. If I displeased you, you could divorce me and still be a rich woman. I know my kingdom is small now, but I have plans. Old Dúnlaing is right to be worried about me. Leinster is weakened after our losses in recent years, but it's still a powerful province—if only someone can unite it. The lands of Muiredach to the south are rich with cattle. He's grown lazy over the years and his kingdom is ripe for conquest. Then there's the territory of Eógan to the east on the sea. His port on the mouth of the Avoca River brings in trade from Britain and Gaul, even Constantinople and Alexandria. Whoever manages those imports properly could be a very wealthy man. Then there's your tribe. They might join me willingly when they see one of their own people standing with me as queen. Dúnlaing's sons certainly don't inspire much confidence. After that there's Munster, a sleeping giant and natural ally against Ulster. We could retake the Boyne Valley that your father gave his life for fighting against those Uí Néill bastards. I could go far, Deirdre, once I have placed my hands on the Stone of Fál and taken the high kingship at Tara. I know that title is worthless now, but I could make it mean something. This whole island could someday be mine, Deirdre, and you could be there beside me."

I always knew Cormac was ambitious, but I had no idea his aspirations were so grand. If he were any other man, I would have laughed at such wild dreams. But I knew if anyone could make them come true, it was Cormac. For a moment I imagined myself as queen of Ireland, dressed in fine royal robes and sipping wine from golden cups. I also imagined the arms of a man holding me again on a long, cold night.

"And of course, you could still worship as you do now," Cormac assured me. "I would help you build churches across Ireland with the monastery of Brigid ruling over them all, including Armagh. Christianity could be a very useful tool for uniting this island. And I wouldn't be like that idiot Fergus you were married to before. I value your independence and intelligence too much. In fact, I'm counting on them. I'm looking for a partner, Deirdre. There would be children, of course, but your sons would be princes, kings someday."

I could barely breathe.

"Deirdre," he said as he took my hand, "do you remember the first time you kissed me?"

"You think I would forget that night under the tree, Cormac?"

"No, not then," he smiled. "It was a dozen years before that. My father had brought me with him to your grandmother's house to ask her advice about something. We were only about four years old. We were playing in the yard and I made you a crown out of flowers. I put it on your head, then you gave me a big kiss and ran back into the hut."

It had been so long ago, but suddenly the memory came rushing back.

"Cormac, I had forgotten. The flowers, they were white clover."

"Yes."

"I hung them on a peg over my bed. They were my first gift from a boy."

"Not gold or jewels, but they were from the heart."

"Oh Cormac, I—"

"Don't give me an answer now, Deirdre. Go back to Kildare and think about it. I'll see you soon. I promise."

I got up from the table and managed a shaky bow to my old friend, the new king of Glendalough. He rose and gave me a gentle, lingering kiss on the lips, then walked out the door.

I wish he'd kissed me longer.

Chapter Fifteen

D ari and I took a different route back to Kildare than the one we had travelled earlier. I wanted to see the body of the man who had carried the Ogam letter. One of Cormac's men had told me they had found nothing else on him except for some unremarkable clothing, a wool blanket, and a simple knife. I don't know what I expected to discover so many weeks later, but I wanted to try.

We hadn't had a chance to talk undisturbed at Cormac's guest house, so as soon as we were out of the valley I told Dari about the letter.

"Deirdre, this is serious. If Dúnlaing's sons are working with the abbot, we're in deep trouble. But does it have to mean they stole the bones?"

"Of course it does. Not them personally, but one of Lorcan's men must have done the deed."

"But the letter doesn't mention the bones, does it?"

"No, but it turned up just before the bones were discovered missing. What else do you think the conspiracy could be about?"

"I don't know, maybe stealing our cattle or killing us all in our sleep. I admit, the letter makes the abbot and the king's son the prime suspects in the theft of the bones, but it doesn't cross anyone off the list. Even Cormac said no one came near the monastery on Michaelmas."

"No band of raiders attacked us, but a single thief could have slipped past Cormac's men that night."

"Assuming his men were really there to protect us. I don't trust Cormac. Are you sure the letter is genuine?"

"Yes, that much I am sure of. Cormac took the oath of a king."

Dari kicked a rock down the trail and scared a rabbit that had been hiding in a gorse bush. If I had a sling, I would have killed it and made us a fresh stew that night.

"Deirdre, you say Cormac swore he didn't forge the letter, but did he swear he didn't take the bones?"

"Well, no, but—"

She was right. During our whole conversation he never actually denied stealing the bones.

"But the letter, Dari, the letter!"

"Like I said, it's proof they're up to something, but those Ogam marks don't say what, do they?"

"Dari, I was having such a good day until I starting talking with you."

We kept walking north. I still wanted to check out the place where the messenger was killed. Cormac said they hadn't buried him, just stripped him and thrown the body into the bushes. It seemed barbaric to Dari, but I wanted to see him. We just had to make sure to stay on the south side of the river away from Illann's farmstead.

The path we took went east of the Wicklow Gap up the slopes of Mullaghcleevaun, one of the highest mountains in the Wicklow range. It wasn't the easiest way, but it was the shortest route to the body. We stopped for a quick lunch at the summit near an old passage tomb and admired the view on that cool, clear day. Far across the eastern sea I could just make out the mountains of Britain. I knew that more Britons were moving into those highlands every year to escape the Saxon invaders who were spreading across the island.

We finished our meal and made our way down the north side of the mountain, stopping at a small spring to drink the cold water bubbling from the rocks.

"I notice you haven't said much about your meeting with Cormac apart from the letter. Did he behave himself?"

"No, Dari, he made wild, passionate love to me on top of his feasting table. I'm surprised you didn't hear us all the way in the guest house."

"I'm serious, Deirdre. What did he say?"

"I'm not sure I want to talk about it yet."

"Really? It must be good."

We walked for a few more minutes in silence.

"Are you ready to talk about it now?"

"Dari, I don't know why people say I'm the nosy one."

"I'm only nosy about you. I can tell you're troubled by more than letters and bones."

"Cormac wants to make me queen of Ireland."

"Is that all? I thought maybe he was going to crown you pope in Rome."

"I'm serious, Dari. He wants me to marry him and help him extend his rule over the whole island."

"You must be joking."

"No, I'm not. He plans to begin with the tribes of Leinster, then ally himself with Munster to bring down the Uí Néill. He wants to use Christianity to unite Ireland, with me by his side."

Dari stopped in the middle of the trail.

"Well, what did you tell him?"

"I didn't tell him anything. I was too shocked to give him an answer. Then he kissed me."

"I take it you don't mean just a friendly kiss."

"It was very friendly. It was soft and warm and—"

"Deirdre, I hate to state the obvious, but you're a nun. You're not supposed to be kissing men like that, even old lovers. Especially old lovers."

"Maybe I don't want to be a nun anymore."

We sat down on a nearby log.

"Deirdre, you are the best friend I've ever had. More than anything in the world, I want you to be happy. If you want to leave the monastery and marry Cormac, I will stand beside you at your wedding and cheer. But please think about what you're doing. I don't think Cormac really loves you, not like you love him. I believe he would treat you well, but he would never give you his heart. Are gold jewelry and royal feasts really worth giving the rest of your life to him?"

"It's not about gold and feasts, Dari. Cormac and I are a good fit. We come from the same background and understand the ways of the nobility. Maybe Cormac won't ever rule over anything more than his valley of Glendalough, but he's eager to try. I admire that kind of ambition in a man, whether he succeeds or not. All Fergus ever wanted was to raise cattle on his little farm and that's fine, but I want more than that, for myself and for any children I might have. Love isn't everything."

We walked for a few minutes past a small waterfall and a patch of yellow ragweed flowering for the last time before winter.

"Deirdre, I know you and I are from different worlds. And it's not just that I'm a commoner. I grew up in a family where there wasn't any kindness or affection. I was married to a husband who cared nothing for me. I'm sure nobility and ambition matter to you, but I would have given anything just to have a good man who truly loved me."

Tears were rolling down her face. I put my arm around her.

"I'm so sorry, Dari. I didn't mean anything by what I said. I'm just being foolish."

"You're not foolish, just honest."

"Dari, you're young and pretty and everybody likes you. There are plenty of decent men around Kildare. Have you ever thought about leaving the monastery and getting married?"

She wiped her tears away and shook her head.

"Deirdre, you know I can't have children. A man could love me with all his heart, but he would still want sons and daughters. It's only natural. And in any case, I like being a nun. I believe in the work we do for the poor and needy. I like singing and praying in the church. I love working with the children and watching them grow up. It's almost like they're my own."

She pulled a rag out of her sleeve and blew her nose, then started off quickly down the trail, calling to me over her shoulder.

"We should get moving if we want to find your dead body before dark."

The spot Cormac's man had described was in a dense forest near a ford on the southern bank of the Liffey. He said the body was in a tall holly bush off the trail next to an oak tree whose trunk had been split by a bolt of lightning. Illann's farm lay a couple of miles across the river in Dúnlaing's tribal lands.

I found the oak tree, then saw the holly bush with its thick prickly leaves and bright red berries. I carefully pushed aside the branches. Dari offered to help, but I could tell she found the whole business ghoulish, so I asked her to go to the river and fill up our water skins instead.

At last I found what was left of the man's body. It was only a skull along with the rib cage and a femur a few feet away. I was surprised there was no smell. Animals had carried away most of the remains and vermin had stripped away the flesh. The leg bone showed bite marks from some large creature, probably a wolf. The skull had a deep indentation above the left eye where one of Cormac's warriors had struck the man with a sword.

I searched all around the holly bush and under the oak tree as well. Any signs of a struggle had long since vanished. Cormac said his guards had chased the man some distance and at last cornered him under the tree. On a whim I peeked inside the broken trunk and saw something glittering deep in the hole. It was a necklace of colored glass on a copper cord, not something a noble lady would wear but good enough for a farm wife. It was an odd thing for a man to carry, as it was something only a woman would own. I felt around in the hole again and found a decorated bronze fibula made for holding a cloak together. The stranger must have known he was trapped and thrown these two items into the tree hoping he could talk his way out of being killed, then retrieve them later. Or maybe he knew he was going to die and didn't want the guards to have them.

"Did you find anything?" Dari asked when she returned with the water sacks.

"Not much. Just a glass necklace and a fibula." I showed them to her.

"Was there anything left of the body?"

"Only a few gnawed bones."

"A long detour for so little."

"Maybe not. It confirms Cormac's story of a man killed in a violent encounter weeks ago just where he said it happened. The fibula is a luxury item, even though the man was dressed in common clothing. That means he received it as a gift from someone wealthy. Then there's the necklace. Why would a man carry a woman's necklace unless he was bringing home a gift for a wife or sweetheart? This unfortunate soul must have travelled to Armagh, traded for the necklace there, then was returning from his errand when he was killed. He must have been a commoner working for a nobleman. And since he was on this path, that nobleman was almost certainly Illann."

"So what are you going to do now? Sneak into Illann's farm and find out if any of his men are missing?"

"Of course not. You and I are going to knock on his door and ask him."

Chapter Sixteen

An hour later the sun was setting and our clothes were still wet from fording the Liffey. We were walking towards the moat and wooden palisade that encircled Illann's farm. Being on the frontier with a sometimes hostile neighboring kingdom, it was more fortified than most compounds. I could see one tall guard at the open gate and another on the watchtower above it.

"This is insane," Dari declared. "After you humiliated him at his father's feast, Illann wants you dead. He knows you're in charge of finding the bones. He knows you think he stole them. Why didn't we just cut our own throats back there in the woods and save him the trouble?"

"Illann wouldn't dare hurt us, Dari. I'm a bard and we're both sisters of holy Brigid. His father would kill him if he laid a hand on us."

"What if his father never finds out? This is an isolated place. Our bones could turn up weeks from now under some holly bush miles from here and Illann would say we must have been set upon by outlaws. No one would believe we were foolish enough to come here alone. I don't believe it myself."

"Have a little faith, Dari, and smile. The guards have seen us."

The man at the gate picked up his spear and called to his companion above to come down. Then they both stood in front of the entrance and waited for us. They didn't look friendly.

"Blessings on you both this fine evening."

"Who are you and what do you want?" the taller one growled.

"I am Sister Deirdre and this is Sister Darerca. We are from the monastery of holy Brigid at Kildare and are subjects of your King Dúnlaing. I am a noblewoman, daughter of the great warrior Sualdam. I am also a bard of the king's court."

I pulled my harp from its case and ran my fingers casually over the strings. They began to look worried. Everyone fears the power of a bard.

"We wish to speak with your lord Illann. Is he in residence?"

The shorter one spoke.

"He—I mean—yes, he's in his feasting hall, but with a guest. Perhaps you could come back another time."

"Gentlemen, we have travelled all day over mountain and glen. The hospitality of your lord is famous throughout Leinster. Do you really want to be responsible for turning away visitors at his gate?"

Before they could answer, I pushed my way through them with Dari close behind. Illann's compound had a barn on the left and sleeping huts on the right. Animal pens held the sheep and cattle that had already been brought in for the night. Storage sheds and other smaller buildings were scattered around the back of the palisade. The feasting hall was in the center. Someone else must have seen us and told Illann of our presence for he was standing at the open door with a frown on his face.

"Illann, blessings upon you. Sister Darerca and I were passing by and we wondered if we might trouble you for a bed in your guest house tonight?"

Dari looked at me with eyes wide. Staying the night was not something we had discussed, but I thought if I pushed Illann enough he might reveal something. I was also hungry and whatever was cooking inside the feasting hall smelled wonderful.

"It would be inhospitable of me to refuse," he said coldly. "I'll have one of my slaves show you to your quarters and bring you some stew."

"You're very kind, but I wonder if we might join you in your feasting hall for just a moment. I have a bit of a puzzle you might be able to help me solve."

The interior of the hut was lit by a small fire with an iron pot hanging over it. Shields and spears lined the walls as well as the desiccated heads of several men with their mouths wide open. Head-hunting had become less common in recent years, but some warriors such as Illann still liked to display the trophies of enemies they had slain in battle. I wasn't surprised to see the guest the guard had spoken of was Ailill, Illann's brother.

"Greetings, Ailill. I'm sorry to disturb you in the middle of your dinner. You remember Sister Darerca, don't you?"

He didn't say a word. Illann called for a servant to bring us both a bowl of beef stew as we sat down on a bench. The stew was delicious, with wild onions and just a hint of rosemary.

"Illann, I won't trouble you long. Sister Darerca and I are on our way back from King Cormac's inauguration at Glendalough and we found ourselves passing near your farm. I told Cormac we might be stopping here for the night.

This last part was a lie, but I wanted Illann to think someone knew we were there. I didn't think he would hurt us, but I wanted to improve our odds.

"You came over Mullaghcleevaun?" he asked. "That's an odd path to take from Glendalough to Kildare."

"I know, but it was such a lovely day and we wanted to see the last of the mountain flowers before winter sets in. In any case, Cormac told us of a stranger his border guards had killed on his lands not far from here. I wanted to look at the body."

At those words, Ailill turned white as a sheet. Even Illann looked uncomfortable.

"We found the remains of the poor man lying in a holly bush near a large oak tree split by lightning," I said. "And I happened to find these hidden inside it."

I handed him the necklace and fibula.

"Since the man was close to your farm and had such a fine fibula, I wondered if he could have been one of your warriors?"

Illann turned the fibula over in the firelight, then examined the necklace briefly. He glanced at Ailill, who was reaching for his sword, and gave his younger brother a quick shake of his head.

"Yes, I know the owner of this fibula, who I presume was carrying the necklace as well, though I've never seen it. His name was Follamain and he was one of my best men. I sent him to the coast a few weeks ago to meet a trading vessel from Britain, but he never returned. I've been wondering if he was taken by slave raiders. The necklace was probably a gift for his wife. I'll see that she gets it."

"Ah, please give her my condolences as well.

Ailill then spoke in his gravelly voice.

"Did you find anything else?"

Illann shot him a stern glance.

"Something else?" I asked. "Such as what, Ailill?"

"I—I don't know," he answered. "Maybe a knife or coins or something."

"Well, nothing valuable. Though Cormac's men did find this."

From my cloak, I pulled the parchment letter with the Armagh seal and handed it to Illann.

As soon as Ailill saw it he pulled out his sword. Dari quickly leapt from her seat with her dinner knife in hand and stood her ground next to me. Illann threw himself between the three of us and grabbed his brother's arm with both his hands.

"No, Ailill!"

"Illann, she—"

"Shut up, Ailill! Sit down and keep your mouth shut! I'll handle this."

Ailill slowly lowered his sword and put it back in its scabbard. Both brothers remained standing, so I rose as well. Dari didn't back down an inch, but she lowered her knife.

"Don't you want to read the message, Illann?" I asked.

He unfolded the parchment and rapidly read the Ogam words. Then he passed it to Ailill, who I could tell was struggling to make out the signs.

"Would you like me to interpret it for you, Ailill?" I asked.

"I can read it myself!"

"So, Illann, you can see why we came to visit. You've confirmed that it was your man who was carrying that message. It provides fairly damning evidence that you were conspiring with the abbot of Armagh to hire Lorcan and do something to Kildare on Michaelmas. I'm going to take a wild guess here, but I bet you were planning to steal the bones of Brigid that night. How am I doing so far?"

I had to admire Illann. I had him trapped, but he forced himself to stay calm.

"Deirdre," Illann said, "you forget to mention that I never received this letter. If the abbot was planning something against Kildare, word never reached me. Perhaps you should go to Armagh and ask him about it."

"Oh come now, Illann." I said. "You expect me to believe the abbot sent a message to you by your own man specifying our monastery, a date, and a notorious outlaw, and this is the first you've heard of it?"

"Yes. Can you prove otherwise?"

"I can talk to your father and tell him what I know."

Ailill started to move toward me again, but Illann stopped him.

"Go ahead and do that, Deirdre. I'll tell him Cormac forged this letter to cause trouble between our kingdoms. Maybe the young king has the bones himself. He used to be your lover, didn't he?"

"Oh, nice try, Illann. Maybe you could tell Dúnlaing that Cormac and I stole the bones together and now we're trying to blame you and your charming brother?"

"Maybe you are," he said. "In any case, your evidence against us is rather weak. I think Sister Anna will tell you that you're going to have to do better."

He clapped his hands and a slave woman appeared.

"Show these two sisters to my guest house. Make sure they have whatever they need."

The woman bowed and motioned us toward the door.

"And Deirdre," Illann said, "I would advise you not to place too much faith in Cormac. You and I may not like each other, but at least you know what kind of man I am."

Chapter Seventeen

I t seems to me, Sister Deirdre, that you have once again accomplished nothing."

I was in Sister Anna's hut after Dari and I had returned from Illann's farm. I had shown the abbess the letter and told her everything Cormac had said to me—well, almost everything.

"But I've found proof that the abbot and Dúnlaing's sons have been conspiring to destroy the monastery. They must have hired Lorcan to steal the bones!"

"Sister Deirdre, where in the letter does it mention bones? And I'm afraid I'm not as impressed as you are by Cormac's royal oath that the letter is genuine. I have little faith in the vaunted nobility of Irish kings, especially Cormac. He lied to me many times when he was a student here in hope of getting out of trouble, but that never stopped me from taking a switch to his back."

"But if the letter is genuine, what else could it be about aside from the bones? It's proof the bones were stolen by a thief hired by the abbot and the king's sons. I don't think Illann would dare to keep the bones here in Leinster for fear his father would find out, so they must be on Lorcan's island or in Armagh."

Sister Anna frowned at me and shook her head.

"Sister Deirdre, you are sorely trying my patience. I repeat, the letter proves nothing. The churchmen of Armagh and the nobles of Dúnlaing have been trying to ruin this monastery since before you were born. I'd be surprised if they haven't been working together for years behind the king's back."

"But Sister—"

"I'm not finished, young lady."

Suddenly I was back in Sister Anna's mathematics class when I was ten years old. No matter how hard I worked, it was never good enough for her.

"Let's assume you're right," she continued, "that the letter is both genuine and its subject is the bones of holy Brigid. What will you do? Go to Lorcan's island and demand them back? All that will gain us is a dead nun. And if the abbot has them in Armagh, do you think he'll just hand them over to you because you asked? You need proof much more solid than this letter to force him to do anything. You need reliable witnesses who can testify before the synod of bishops that the abbot has the bones. That is our only hope of getting them back."

"Sister Anna, we tried to find witnesses. I don't know where else to look. I'm doing my very best."

"Then may heaven help us, because it isn't good enough. It's been a month since the bones have gone missing and what have you found? A ribbon, a cross, and a dubious letter—but not the bones. Need I remind you that no pilgrims have visited Kildare recently, our food stores are shrinking every day, and I received another gracious note from the abbot this morning offering to help us in exchange for selling him our souls. I don't need excuses from you, I need the bones!"

I left Sister Anna's hut and went back to my quarters. There I knelt by my bed, crossed myself, and pounded on my mattress until my fists hurt. What did that woman want from me?

Father Ailbe was standing by the door when I came out.

"So, my child, did you or the mattress win?"

"Abba, I'm sorry." I put my head on his shoulder. "I'm just so frustrated. Sister Anna expects miracles."

We sat down on the bench outside the church. The last rays of the sun were fading in the west.

"She has high expectations, certainly, but you have extraordinary abilities."

"Not extraordinary enough for her. I thought I was making real progress."

I told him everything that had happened while I was away, about the letter, and about my conversation with Cormac, even the part about the kiss. He was quiet for a while, then spoke.

"Cormac is a remarkable young man with great talents. He would be a worthy match for you. What do you want to do?"

"I don't know, Abba. I would never want to leave you and Dari, but let's face it, I'm a terrible nun. There are times when I even wonder if I even believe in God. Does that make me a bad Christian?"

"No, it makes you human. Being a Christian doesn't mean being free from doubt, it means having faith in spite of doubts."

"Faith is hard. Abba, I'm sure your life hasn't always been easy. How have you been such a good Christian all these years?"

He gave me a wry smile.

"My child, if you knew all the sins I've committed, you wouldn't think I'm a good Christian at all."

He got up slowly from the bench and held out his hand to me.

"We'd better get moving. Sister Anna will be angry at both of us if we're late for evening prayers."

I decided to spend the next two weeks revisiting the farms and homes around Kildare questioning everyone again. Sister Anna wanted witnesses that the abbot and Dúnlaing's sons had engineered the theft of the bones and I was determined to find them for her.

My last visit was the one I had been putting off as long as possible. I arrived at the farm of Fergus in the morning so there would be no question of me spending the night. As soon as I walked through the gate, Boann's son Tigernach ran up and gave me a big hug.

"Tiger, you've grown a foot since I saw you last. How old are you now, eleven?"

"I'm twelve, Deirdre," he said proudly, puffing out his chest. "Did my father tell you I killed a buck last month? I've got the head mounted above my bed."

"So I heard. That's wonderful, Tiger. You're going to be fighting off the girls before you know it."

He blushed and led me to his mother's hut where Boann was nursing one of her twins.

"Deirdre, welcome!" Boann was a tall, powerful woman with flaming red hair. She always reminded me of some warrior woman out of Irish legend.

She passed the baby to one of her older daughters and gave me a firm embrace. Ness, the other wife of Fergus, was there as well and hugged me till I thought I would pop. Ness was a black-haired beauty with eyes as dark as a seal. Some people whispered that her grandmother had been a selkie from the sea near Inishmore.

"What brings you here, Deirdre?' asked Ness as she handed me a bowl of porridge.

"Monastery business, I'm afraid. Sister Anna has put me in charge of finding the missing bones of Brigid, though I'm not having much luck. I'm questioning everyone again hoping to find some clue we missed before. I think the bones were stolen sometime around Michaelmas at the end of September. Did either of you see anything unusual then, any strangers passing through the woods or fields?"

"I was in labor then," Ness said, "and wasn't paying much attention to anything else."

"And I was with her the whole time," said Boann. "Besides, I was so busy being pregnant with the twins, the whole Uí Néill army could have invaded and I wouldn't have noticed."

We all laughed. It was good to talk with them again just like in the old days.

"Was Fergus around then?" I asked.

"Oh yes," said Boann. "He was so worried about us he didn't stray from the farm until a few days after the twins were born when he snuck off in the night by himself. He claimed he was going hunting, but I think he just wanted some peace and quiet. Men are useless around babies in any case."

"Was he gone long?"

"No, he was back by dawn," said Ness.

"Is he here now?" I asked.

"I think he's out behind the barn mending a plow on the forge. I can send Tiger to find out."

"No need," I said as I got up. "I just want to talk with him for a minute."

I walked across the familiar farmyard past my old hut, now empty. The flower garden I had planted in front had turned to dust. I think Fergus was using the hut now to store cattle feed.

When I came to the empty bull pen next to the barn, I stopped and leaned against the wooden fence. This was the last place in the world I wanted to linger, but I couldn't help myself. I stood there alone and remembered.

When I was in my early twenties, there were plenty of men in my life, any one of whom would have made a good husband. Almost all of them asked if they could pay a bride price to my grandmother. One of them offered ten cows with their calves if I would be his wife—an outrageously high price even for someone of my status. But although I enjoyed their company, I had no desire to marry. My work and friendships were enough for me. I was a respected bard who earned rich gifts from patrons as I sung of their glorious ancestors or their own victories in battle. I often accompanied my grandmother on her rounds through the farms of Leinster and saw to the visitors who were always knocking at the door of our home. I read Homer and Virgil with Father Ailbe late into the night. I would also go with him as he made sick calls at households around Kildare or simply sit with him by the fire and listen to his endless tales of faraway places. I had many friends in our tribe and beyond, most of whom I had known since we were children. We would talk and laugh and sing while we passed babies around. It was a rich and full life that I thought was enough for me.

But still I knew that something was missing. By the time I was twenty-five, my friends had all long since married and started families. I loved playing with their children and telling them tales of Irish or Greek heroes. It wasn't so much that I wanted a husband—men are more trouble than they're worth, my grandmother always claimed—but I came to realize that I very much wanted a child of my own.

It was then that Fergus walked into my life. He was a moderately prosperous cattle breeder I had known for years. He was several years older than me with two wives already and half a dozen adorable children. He was a head taller than most men and handsome enough with his big, drooping mustache. He could also be quite charming when he wasn't going on endlessly about the best qualities to look for in breeding stock. He wasn't a Christian, and may not have been my ideal choice for a mate, but he was convenient.

He was visiting my grandmother one summer afternoon seeking her advice about the purchase of a new pasture. She had just talked him out of it when I returned from a wedding and sat down with them both to share a jar of cool wine. By the last cup I was in a jolly mood and asked Fergus if he wanted some company as he rode home. My grandmother raised her eyebrows, but said nothing. I rode behind Fergus on his horse holding him around the waist and listened to him talk about all his children and how they made him laugh. By the time we reached his home it was dark so he invited me to spend the night. His two wives were not the jealous sort and welcomed me. They each had their own hut in the compound where they lived with their children. Fergus took turns going back and forth between them, but that evening he stayed with me. By morning, I knew I wanted to marry him.

When I told my grandmother, she said little. She knew I wanted a child and was not going to stand in my way. She was smart enough not to tell me that Fergus was the wrong man for me because she knew I wouldn't listen. He brought her five fine cows as my bride price. The wedding itself was a small affair at our home with Father Ailbe presiding. When it was done, my grandmother placed my hand in his and gave us her blessing. Then I hugged her and rode away with Fergus.

Marriage wasn't so bad, at least at first. I had my own hut and continued my life much as before. I came and went as I pleased on my bardic rounds. Fergus was happy that I did so since it increased his prestige, and because I was now bringing my earnings home to him. He visited me often at night to perform his husbandly duties, which I have to admit he was quite good at. Before the beginning of winter, I knew I was pregnant.

The other two wives of Fergus were good company and gave me all sorts of helpful advice as I grew ever larger. My trips away became less frequent as travel became more difficult. Other women might go on about how much they enjoy being pregnant, but I felt exhausted and ever more uncomfortable. It once took me five minutes just to bend down and pick up a knife I had dropped. Fergus laughed at me and said I was spoiled having come to childbearing so late. I could have strangled him.

During labor I swore no man would ever touch me again, but I forgot everything when I saw the face of my son for the first time. He opened his eyes and looked at me when the midwife laid him on my chest. He had red hair and eyes the color of a mountain lake. I named him Aidan. As I nursed him that evening in my hut and held him in my arms, I was the happiest woman in the world.

My little boy grew so fast I could hardly believe it. Soon he was crawling around our home and getting into everything. I was jealous when his father visited and made him laugh by playing games with him or doing bird imitations, but I was glad Fergus took such an interest in my contribution to his growing family.

I'm ashamed to confess I began to lose interest in my husband once my son was born. I started to see a hundred things about him that annoyed me. As the months went by, my visits to my grandmother's home with Aidan became longer and more frequent, so much so that Fergus began to grow angry with me for not being with him. Two or three times he struck me, but I just glared at him, daring him to do enough damage for me to go to the brehon judges and divorce him.

When Aidan was just a little over a year old he made his first hesitant steps and ventured outside our hut at Fergus' farm with me at his side. He loved to visit the animal pens and feed the pigs we kept behind the barn. I always worried about him getting hurt, but Fergus said I needed to let the boy have some fun.

One day when Aidan and I returned to the farm from my grandmother's house, I saw that Fergus had bought a new bull. It was a dark red beast, unlike the mostly black cattle he kept. It was enormous and stamped the ground menacingly whenever anyone came near. There was something about that bull that frightened me the first time I saw it. I told Fergus that it had an evil spirit and he should get rid of it, but he just laughed and asked what a woman knew about bulls.

It was only a few days later while I was making supper that I looked up and saw that Aidan wasn't by the fire where I had left him. I usually paid better attention, but I had burned some onions and was trying to scrape them off the bottom of the pan when I saw he was gone. I dropped everything and ran out the door, frantic to find him. He was nowhere in sight, but then I heard the bull in the corral snorting and pawing the earth. My heart stopped beating and I ran to the fence only to see the monster charging my little boy who had somehow crawled under the railing. I screamed and rushed at the bull waving my arms to distract it, but it was too late.

After the servants had dragged the bull away, I held the broken body of my son in my arms and kissed him, as if I could will the life back into him. The rest of the household gathered around me in silence, as Fergus knelt beside me and gently put his hand on my shoulder. I wouldn't look at him. I took my son back to our hut and placed him in his little cot beside my bed along with the toy rabbit he loved so much. I lay beside him all night wondering why I still had breath in my own body.

The next morning we buried him in a nearby grove as I sang a song of lamentation over his grave. Then I walked back to my hut with my harp, wrapped my traveling cloak around my shoulders, and left everything behind.

I stayed with my grandmother for the next two months. Sometimes I would lie in bed for days staring at the roof. Sometimes I would walk down to the stream and watch the leaves float past. Fergus tried to see me several times, but I wanted nothing to do with him. Father Ailbe came and sat with me in silence, knowing I didn't want to talk.

At last my grandmother spoke to me one evening and said I needed to make a decision. My son had passed on to the next life and nothing I could do would bring him back. I needed to go on living, as painful as that might be. She would help me however she could, but I had to find the strength inside myself to do it.

I knew she was right. The next morning I set off down the path to the monastery. I couldn't go back to my old life as a bard living with my grandmother. I wouldn't return to Fergus as much as he wanted me. So I chose the only other world that was familiar to me. I took vows in the church of Kildare and put on the veil as a sister of holy Brigid.

I left the bull pen and found Fergus behind the barn pumping the bellows while he held the glowing blade of the plow in the fire. He was stripped to the waist and covered with sweat in spite of the cool morning. He reminded me of the god Vulcan in his workshop. He looked up as I approached. He didn't seem surprised to see me, but he didn't look pleased either.

"I was wondering when you'd come by. I heard you were making the rounds of all the farms asking questions. Any luck yet?"

"No. I still haven't found the bones."

"Here, pump this." He placed my hand on the bellows handle. I took off my cloak and worked the wooden shaft up and down while Fergus pounded the blade with his hammer. When he plunged the red metal into a bucket of water, it hissed like meat on a spit. Then he motioned me to a bench and sat down next to me. The smell of his sweat reminded me of one hot summer night when we had made love under the stars.

"Fergus, I don't suppose you've heard anything?"

"Maybe, but I'm not sure what it means."

"What was it?"

"A friend of mine was talking to a friend of his from Glendalough who heard that your old boyfriend Cormac was talking with some outlaws in the dead of night a couple of weeks ago. Seems like a strange thing for him to do."

"Were these outlaws Lorcan's men?"

"No, local scum I think."

Cormac had told me he was talking with bandits who knew Lorcan, so this didn't seem strange. I told Fergus about the letter found on the dead man and Cormac's plans to talk to outlaws who might be able to help.

"Hmm, maybe," he said. "I still don't trust him. No king ever did me any favors."

Fergus got up and walked a few steps away. I could tell he was trying to work up the nerve to say something to me.

"I don't want to beat a dead horse, Deirdre, but, like I said before, you can always come back here if the monastery doesn't make it. I could have your old hut cleaned out in a few days. I could fix up the garden so you could plant some more flowers in the spring. I know Boann and Ness would enjoy your company again. So would I."

"Fergus, seriously, what's going on?" I asked. "Why are you so eager to get me back?"

He looked down at the ground as he spoke.

"Deirdre, I meant what I said back at the monastery. I do love you, but there's more to it than that. Last winter was hard for me. I lost six cows and ten calves. Then the barley crop this fall was poor and I had to give up my lease on the land near the river. I even had to sell my last two slaves. I don't have much grain left in storage and if things don't change soon I'm going to have to hire myself out to work for one of Dúnlaing's men. I've been a free farmer all my life, as was my father and his father before me. I don't mind hard work, but I don't want to spend the winter staring at the ass-end of some rich man's sheep just to feed my family. I've got nine children on the farm now with the three babies born this autumn. I don't want them crying because their bellies are empty. I'll do whatever I have to do to take care of them, but it would be a great help if you were back with us. The payments you could bring in as a bard could see us through until summer. I know I'll be alright then. I just need a few months to get back on my feet."

I knew Fergus was having a hard time, everyone was, but I didn't realize things were so bad for him. Still, I had to end this and the only way I knew was to be brutally honest with him.

"Fergus, I appreciate how hard things are for you. Maybe I could get a few chickens from my grandmother and bring them by, for the sake of the children. But let me say this again—*our marriage is over.* It doesn't matter what happens at the monastery, you are no longer my husband and I am never coming back to you. I don't love you. I'm not sure I ever did."

For a long moment he looked like I'd punched him in the stomach. Then he was in front of me with fire in his eyes. He grabbed me by the front of my tunic and lifted me off the ground with one hand and held me against the wall of the barn.

"You're never going to find those bones, Deirdre. You want to starve to death when the monastery closes? Fine by me. I gave you a chance. Keep your damn chickens. I won't let my children go hungry. I'll work all winter long shoveling pig manure for one of Dúnlaing's pretty boys if I have to. I don't need you. I don't want you."

He threw me down on the ground.

"Now get off my farm."

I got up, brushed the dirt off my cloak, and spat on the ground in front of him.

"Go to hell, Fergus."

Then I turned and walked away.

I was eager to get back to Kildare, but I knew I had to make one last stop. It was a place I hadn't been to for over three years. It had been too painful before. I walked down a short path past a field of barley stubble. There, beneath a willow tree on the edge of the farm, far from the noise of children and cattle, I found the tiny grass-covered mound ringed with stones and topped by a small cross.

I knelt and placed my hands gently on the grave, then gave myself over to tears. For what may have been hours, I lay on top of the mound. Then, as the sun began to set, I took out my harp and sang his favorite lullaby:

> Sleep in peace, my darling,
> Sleep in peace, my love.

With a final kiss to the warm ground beneath me, I gathered myself together, and walked back to the monastery.

Chapter Eighteen

C hristmas was only three weeks away and the wind was colder than ever. The monastery was still feeding all the widows and needy who came to us, but the porridge was getting thin. We had bread only twice a week now and meat was just a pleasant memory. I knew we couldn't go on like this. If pilgrims didn't return to Kildare soon with their gifts of food, we might not even make it to holy Brigid's day at the beginning of February. We were hungry now—soon we would be starving.

So I made a decision. I had found no witnesses to the theft of the bones in my search of the farms around Kildare. Nobody had seen anything. It seemed pointless to go to Armagh and confront the abbot, at least not until I had better proof that he was responsible. That left only one possibility open to me.

I had heard nothing more from Cormac about his attempts to contact Lorcan. If the pirate leader had the bones on his island, the only way I was going to get them back was to go there myself and ask for them.

I admit, the prospect terrified me. I had never heard of anyone actually seeking Lorcan out before. Indeed, most people avoided him like the plague—and for good reason. Unlike the lovable scoundrels of Irish legend, real outlaws were ruthless men who didn't take kindly to people knocking on their doors. I knew visiting his camp would be dangerous, but I had confidence that my status as a bard and a nun would protect me.

I didn't tell anyone what I was planning. I couldn't bring myself to say goodbye to my grandmother or Father Ailbe for fear I would burst into tears. I didn't even tell Dari where I was going. As far as they would know, I would still be searching the farms around Kildare.

I thought about wearing my best robes embroidered in gold to impress Lorcan and remind him that I was a poet of the highest rank, a member of a noble, untouchable family of druids. But I finally decided to take a more subtle approach and bring only my harp as a sign of my office. I chose my most tattered nun's robe and no ornament other than my plain wooden cross. I hoped Lorcan might respect me as a Christian sister of holy Brigid, though I had my doubts. Outlaws worshipped Crom Crúach and other dark gods and cared little for the beliefs of others.

At sunrise with my harp and satchel, I headed east, trusting in God. Towards evening I passed a remote lake with a small island in it that I had seen several times before but had never visited. Old stories said that no one on that island could ever die. In ages past, it was said desperate souls would journey from across Ireland to the place. People burdened with age and illness would spend the last of their treasure and strength to travel there and lie down on its cold rocks. But although no one would perish on that island, no one was ever healed either. The sick and diseased continued as they were, in pain and misery, day after endless day. All of them in time begged the ferryman to take them back across the water so they could die in peace and end their suffering.

That night, as I sat by my fire under a moonless sky, I wondered what kind of reception I would receive from Lorcan and his pirates. As I thought about it, I realized I had never met an outlaw before, though I had once seen three of them beheaded by King Dúnlaing for cattle theft.

Outlaws were renegades from Irish society who rejected everything the tribal system stood for. They lived by hunting, plundering, and hiring themselves out to the highest bidder. People called them *ambue* or cowless men since they cared nothing for the traditional measure of wealth and status. Sometimes they were known as the *cú glas* or grey dogs of Ireland since they were more animal than human. Some people said they could even turn themselves into wolves. They had broken all ties with families and tribe to set out on their own. Often they formed into groups for protection from the outside world and to better carry out their work. For an outlaw band, there were no rules except the survival of the strongest. They had no loyalty to anyone, even their own leaders, and were kept in line only through cruelty and intimidation.

And I was on my way to see the most vicious outlaw of all.

On the morning of my third day from Kildare, I climbed to the top of a hill near the eastern coast. In the distance was Lambay, a small island a little over a mile offshore. It had cliffs on three sides where sea birds nested in the spring. Before the pirates came, local farmers had collected eggs there and left their ewes on the island to give birth away from mainland predators. But that was many years ago.

What had started as a clear morning quickly turned cold and grey as I walked down the overgrown trail. Fog rolled in from the sea and a light rain began to fall. I pulled my cloak over my head and prayed as I walked, calling on all the saints in heaven, especially Brigid, to watch over me that day.

The sea was calm as I came to the rocky shore. The water was a beautiful shade of greenish-blue. There were no homes on the coast that I could see. I wasn't surprised that no one wanted to live so close to pirates, but I needed to find someone to take me across to the island. At last I came upon a small hut above a narrow cove with a path leading down to the sea. At the bottom of the path was an old man sitting on a rock mending a currach. Another like it was pulled up onto the beach near him.

I had seen currachs before when I visited my uncle on the Aran Islands. They are small boats made from cowhides stretched over a wicker framework and tightly sewn together. They can leak terribly if they aren't tended properly and are devilishly hard to steer since they lack a keel. The currach this man had was old, made for no more than two people with loops of rope on the sides to hold the oars in place.

"Blessings upon you, Grandfather," I called out in the traditional greeting for elders as I approached him.

He stared at me with hard, narrow eyes. He had only a horrid scar where his nose had once been.

"Who are you? What do you want?"

"I am a bard and a sister of the order of holy Brigid at Kildare. I come on business of my monastery seeking passage to the island so that I might speak with Lorcan."

When he spoke again I could see that most of his teeth were gone.

"No one goes to that island. Only a fool would sail the seas around here."

"But you sail here."

"Then I must be a fool." He looked quickly out at the sea. The fog had covered the strait between the mainland and the island.

"Listen to me, young lady. I don't know what you think you're doing, but if you value your life you will turn around right now and go back to where you came from. You're lucky the fog rolled in, otherwise those damn pirates might have spotted you by now and be on their way to take you. They do nasty things to trespassers, especially women."

"Then why do they allow you to fish here?"

"Because I'm old and poor. I've got nobody left to care whether I live or not. I don't much care myself. Those pirates destroyed everything I ever cared about."

It took him a long time before he could continue.

"My daughter—she was twelve, only twelve years old. She wasn't even pledged to a man yet. Those animals took her when they first came here years ago and made her a slave on the island. I tried to ransom her, but they laughed when they saw all I had was a basket of fish. They wouldn't even let me see her. I tried to sneak over there a few nights later and rescue her, but they caught me and did this." He pointed to his nose.

"Then they tied me to a pole and brought out my little girl. She screamed when she saw what they had done and tried to reach me, but they knocked her down in the mud. They raped her there in front of me, four or five of the beasts, while I tore at my ropes and cursed them. When they were done, they slit her throat."

He sat down on a rock.

"They let me go so I could tell others what they did. When my wife saw me and heard the story, she was in my boat before I could stop her and was rowing across to the island with a kitchen knife. They killed her too."

He turned to look at me.

"That was over thirty years ago. I've lived here alone ever since and have never been back to the island. So listen to me and get away from here now. They won't care that you're a bard. You think your harp or that cross around your neck will protect you? They won't."

I sat with him for a long time on that rock.

Did I really want to risk speaking with Lorcan? Even if he had the bones, were they worth my life? But I knew in my heart that without the bones, everything Brigid had dreamed of, all we had worked for, would come to an end. People were depending on me. Didn't I believe God would protect and watch over me—or were those just empty words I prayed?

"I know you're trying to keep me safe from harm, but I must get to that island."

He shook his head again.

"I won't take you there."

"But that's where I must go and you have the only boat on this coast."

I stood up.

"I am a bard from an ancient line of bards. I come from a family of powerful druids and noble warriors. I command you by the authority of King Dúnlaing to take me to that island."

He looked amused.

"I don't care if the queen of the fairy people sent you, I'm not taking you."

"Alright then, loan me one of your boats. I'll row myself."

He gave a snort. "Child, have you ever rowed a currach before? You'll end up going in circles or getting swept out to sea—which would be a better fate than what waits for you on that island."

"Yes, I've rowed boats like yours many times." Well, at least a few times. Maybe twice. "I can handle myself. Just give me the oars."

At last he shrugged and got up. He retrieved two oars from behind a rock and brought them to me, then helped me launch the boat into the water. I climbed in and fixed the oars.

"Grandfather, I thank you for your kindness. I'll bring the boat back soon. Please don't worry about me."

He shook his head one last time. "I wish I could change your mind, but I can see you're a stubborn one. My wife was stubborn too."

With that he pushed me out to sea.

I had trouble steering the boat at first, but soon fell into the rhythm of rowing. A bigger problem was keeping my course in the fog that soon enveloped me. My only guide was the dim glow of the sun to the south, but I knew if I kept that to my left I would reach the island.

I must have been halfway there when a strange sight appeared off the bow of the boat. It was a small flock of puffins floating on the water, all watching me in silence. It was odd to see puffins that time of year. By then they were usually well out to sea where they wintered. I was always amazed they could fly with their dumpy black and white bodies, but they nested on high cliffs along the coast.

The fog grew even thicker after an hour of rowing. I knew I must be drawing near the island, but it wasn't until I felt the boat scrape bottom that I knew I had reached the beach. I had been expecting watchmen, but there were none. The boats of the pirates lay empty nearby. I pulled the currach up onto the shore and took out my satchel. The silence was unnerving and I began to wonder if the outlaws were lying in wait for me behind a rock. With a final prayer and my heart pounding like a drum, I walked up the path towards what I hoped was the hut of Lorcan.

I remembered the story of the Roman hero Aeneas sneaking into an enemy city surrounded by a divine mist.

Like him I passed unseen through the fog into the heart of the pirate camp.

Suddenly there was a wooden post in front of me and I could barely stifle a scream. There was the body of a man tied to it. His hands had been chopped off. He hadn't been dead long, but the crows had already picked out his eyes. I kept walking.

At last I came to a large circular hut made of the usual wattle and daub with a thick thatch roof. I could smell peat burning inside and hear the gruff voices of men. There were skulls attached to the outside of the doorpost and no bench for visitors, as was the custom in Irish homes. I took a deep breath and tried to stop my hands from shaking. I decided that if I was going to make a proper impression I had better do this right. I took out my harp and held it to my chest. Without knocking I threw open the door and marched inside.

I took in the room at a glance. There was a hearth fire in the middle with some kind of large animal roasting over it on a spit. Around the fire were about twenty of the most despicable-looking men I had ever seen. Most of them looked like they could casually rip the head off a horse. Some had scars on their faces and several were missing ears. They all wore gold torques and jeweled necklaces. If they weren't drunk already they were well on their way.

All of them fell silent and turned to stare at me as I entered. There were two or three slave women with disheveled hair carrying food and wine to the men. On the walls were what seemed to be trophies—decorated iron swords, golden torques, silver plates. At the front of the room in a chair covered with a lion's skin was an older man with a goblet in his hand. He was looking at me with great curiosity.

"My name is Deirdre," I said loudly. "I am a one of the sisters of holy Brigid from the monastery at Kildare. I am also a bard and a member of the Order. I wish to speak to Lorcan."

No one said anything for a moment. Then the man sitting on the lion-skin chair spoke.

"Welcome, Deirdre. I am Lorcan, leader of this group of gentlemen. Please come closer so I can see you better."

I moved to the open space between his chair and the fire. This close to Lorcan I could see he was a man of average height, about fifty years old with long grey hair woven into braids. His beard was braided as well. He wore a simple brown tunic and woolen pants with short leather boots. He wore no jewelry. I noticed that one of his eyes was blue and the other green. He was smiling and seemed almost pleased to see me.

"Would you like some wine, Deirdre? Perhaps something to eat?" he asked.

"Thank you, my lord. A cup of wine would be most welcome after my journey." I decided it was best to be polite. I was expecting a coarse ruffian. It was unnerving to have him act so courteously.

He snapped his fingers and one of the women brought wine for me in a golden goblet and a stool for me to sit on.

"You've traveled a long way from Kildare to see me. What can I do for you?"

My mouth had suddenly gone dry, so I drained the cup.

"My lord, perhaps you've heard that the bones of holy Brigid were stolen from the church at Kildare. These bones are worthless in themselves, but they draw many pilgrims to our monastery in search of hope and healing. We would very much like to get them back. You are a powerful man in Ireland. I was hoping that perhaps you could help me."

He then gave me the most charming smile.

"My dear, I have indeed heard about the theft of the bones. I make it my business to know about such things throughout the four provinces."

"Then, my lord, you should know that the sisters of holy Brigid would be willing to negotiate for their return. I'm certain we could come to a mutually beneficial arrangement."

He signaled the slave woman to refill my wine glass.

"There are many thieves in Ireland, Sister Deirdre, but I do insist on being involved in such activities. I can be rather severe when someone tries to cut me out. Perhaps you saw the unfortunate man tied to the post as you came in? That was my favorite nephew, a misguided youth who stole a hoard of silver coins from a merchant. He tried to hide the theft and not give me my accustomed share. I had him brought back here for punishment. A pity, really. He was such a nice boy."

I felt a chill run down my spine, but I pressed on, carefully.

"My lord, I had heard that perhaps the abbot of the monastery at Armagh and the two sons of King Dúnlaing might have approached you about acquiring the bones for them."

"Sister Deirdre, I don't usually discuss business with parties not involved, but I'll make an exception in your case."

He took a long draft of wine from his cup.

"The abbot and Dúnlaing's sons did indeed approach me about hiring my services to steal the bones from your monastery."

I knew it! I knew I was right about the letter and about the bones. Now I could get them back. If Lorcan didn't have them there on the island, then he must have given them to the abbot. I could go to Armagh and demand their return. The synod of bishops would strip him of his office and send him into exile. Or maybe they would let him stay at Armagh tending pigs.

"The representative from the abbot and the king's sons came to me over two months ago," he continued. "But I declined their request."

No. Lorcan had to have taken the bones. Why was he telling me this? Was he trying to mislead me?

"It's not that I have any reservations about stealing from holy places, Christian or druid," he said, "but I had an encounter with Brigid when I was a young man that gave me pause.

"I was working as a sheep thief near Kildare in those days, always on the lookout for an easy target. I had heard Brigid often tended her own flocks, so I crept up on her pasture one spring day. I counted fifty sheep on the hillside, most of them ewes but a good number of castrated males as well. I spirited away a fat wether before she even knew I was there. I led it to a pen I had built about half a mile away and then came back for another. I thought at first she must have been blind not to see me, but then a strange feeling came over me, as if perhaps she knew exactly what I was doing and was deliberately ignoring me. But I kept on all day and by evening I had seven animals in my pen. I snuck back to Brigid's flock that evening and followed her to her fold just to watch her surprise when the foolish woman found seven of her sheep missing. She counted them loudly as each one entered the gate. When the last one came through, she tapped it with her staff and turned to look at the bushes where I was hiding and shouted, "fifty." I couldn't believe it. I counted them myself three times and found she was right. Not a single sheep was missing. I was so struck by this magic I left my hiding place and retrieved the sheep I had stolen from her. I returned them to her and begged her forgiveness. She smiled and told me to count the sheep again, including those I had brought back. I did and to my amazement there were still fifty in all.

"So you see, although I fear neither god nor man, I have the greatest respect for Brigid and would not dare to disturb her resting bones."

My shoulders sank. I had been so hopeful that Lorcan would have the bones and all of our troubles would be over. He rose from the chair and came to stand before me, putting his hand on my arm like a father comforting a daughter.

"I am sorry I couldn't help you, Deirdre. I know how frustrating it must be for you to have come all this way for nothing."

I stood up.

"You have been most gracious, my lord. I thank you for your hospitality. With your permission, I will leave you gentlemen to finish your dinner."

Lorcan smiled and looked at me kindly.

"My dear, what makes you think you're going to leave this room alive?"

I froze.

"What do you mean?"

"I'm sorry, Deirdre, but I have something of a reputation to maintain. You know, vicious pirate and all that. If I allow you to live, my men might think I've grown soft."

He motioned for a couple of his men to come and stand beside me. They looked about eight feet tall. I could feel the heat from their bodies.

"But my lord, I am a woman, a sister of holy Brigid, and a bard of the highest rank."

"Yes, my dear, I know. I've had to kill many women over the years. Regrettable, but necessary. Regarding religion, doesn't your god honor those who die in his name? Perhaps I would be doing you a favor. And as for being a bard, I kidnapped one last year and unfortunately had to drown him. I have his harp in my treasury. Would you like to see it?"

"No, thank you, my lord."

I was thinking as furiously as I ever had in my life. There must be a way I could get out of this. But standing face to face with this pirate, my mind was a blank.

And then it hit me. Face to face. Outlaws rejected all the traditions and constraints of Irish society except one. They valued their *enech*, their face, their reputation above all. Lorcan had said it himself, he had a reputation to maintain.

"My lord," I said calmly, "you are a great leader of outlaws, known throughout Ireland and beyond. Men whisper your name in fear and kings dread the sight of your ships on their shores."

"Indeed?" he smiled. "It's so gratifying to have my work appreciated."

"When you capture someone, whether man, woman, or child, you prove your skill and daring to all. You take whomever you wish by stealth, guile, and courage, doing with them as you will. If they die at your hands, it is a fate to be expected. The stronger beast stalks his prey and devours it. That is the way of the world."

"True enough. But what does that have to do with you?"

He motioned his men to hold my arms as he drew his dagger from his belt.

"My lord," I spoke so the whole room could hear me clearly. "I am a woman, alone and unarmed. I have come to your island of my own accord. I have walked into your hall without a sword at my back. If I were taken in a raid and brought here to die, I would be just another victim. But I came here freely and stand before you unbound. Where is the honor for you in my death? What will your men say? Has the lion grown too weak for the hunt?"

Lorcan looked at me closely for a long time. He seemed as if he were about to strike. I could feel the grip of his men tighten on my arms.

Then he laughed.

"Deirdre, you are a most clever woman. You're right, of course. Where's the sport in killing someone I didn't trap myself?"

He spoke to his men.

"Let her go."

The two giants released me. Lorcan slipped his knife back in its sheath.

"Now, my dear, I would advise you to leave my little island quickly and not return. If I catch you some day in one of my snares, you will meet a very different fate."

I bowed to him and turned toward the door. The eyes of every man in the room followed me as I left. I went down the path again to the beach and climbed into the boat, then rowed away as fast as I could through the lifting fog.

Chapter Nineteen

Y ou did what?"
I had just told Dari about my trip to Lorcan's island. I had never seen her so angry.

"Deirdre, truly, have you lost your mind or do you have some kind of death wish?"

She was stomping up and down the floor of our sleeping quarters. Thankfully no one else was around.

"Dari, calm down. I'm fine."

"Calm down? Deirdre, you just went to see the most dangerous, bloodthirsty man in Ireland and barely escaped with your life and you want me to calm down?"

"I'm sorry. I know it was reckless, but I was desperate to find the bones. I really thought they were on Lorcan's island. And I thought being a bard and a nun would protect me."

"Deirdre, you are my best friend and I love you, but this is too much. The bones of Brigid are important, but they are not worth your life!"

"Please don't worry, Dari. I promise I won't take any chances like that again. It was foolish, I know, but I was just trying to help save the monastery. Please forgive me. And please don't tell anyone what I did, especially Father Ailbe or my grandmother."

"Oh, I'd love to see what your grandmother would do if she found out! That would be a fitting punishment."

"Dari, please!"

"Fine, Deirdre. But if you ever do anything like this again, I swear I will tell her and everyone else. I mean it."

She stormed out of the hut and slammed the door behind her. I couldn't really blame her for being so angry. If the roles had been reversed, I would have been furious.

But in spite of the harrowing experience on Lorcan's island, I had learned something important. The abbot and Dúnlaing's sons had indeed tried to hire the outlaw king to steal the bones of Brigid. The letter Cormac's men found must have been instructions to Illann and Ailill about how and when the theft would take place. Whoever the abbot had used to contact Lorcan had been rebuffed by the pirate sometime after he sent the letter to Illann's sons, but the abbot wouldn't give up that easily. He must have arranged for someone else to steal the bones when Lorcan rejected him, but who?

I decided the only path I had left to me was to go to Armagh and confront the abbot himself. Maybe one of the sisters there had seen something and could help me. Dari had grown up with a couple of the Armagh nuns, so I would take her along. Even if the sisters there couldn't help, I had no choice but to go to the abbot. He had to have the bones. There was nowhere else they could be. But how could I force the abbot to confess?

There was no way I could get Lorcan to testify against him to the bishops—he had only told me about the abbot's plan because he expected to kill me before I left his island. Maybe I could threaten the abbot with a satire? He was part of an old Irish royal family. The power of a bard might still mean something to him. If that didn't work, I was prepared to do whatever was necessary to get the bones back from Armagh. I would just have to figure it out when I got there.

The next day it began to snow. This wasn't so strange, since almost every year we would get a flurry in December or January, though by the next day it would always melt and the pastures would be green again. But this time the snow didn't stop or melt since the temperature never rose above freezing. For three days it continued to fall until there was at least a foot on the ground. I decided to postpone my trip to Armagh for a few days. Travel would be impossible with the roads covered in snow.

I remembered the opening lines of a song my grandfather had written:

> Listen to the stags bellowing.
> It snows in winter,
> summer is gone.

For the first week everyone thought the snow was pretty, with the buildings of the monastery covered in a blanket of white and the bare trees outlined with frost. I enjoyed hearing the crunch beneath my feet and watching the children play in what was such a novelty to all of us. But the animals quickly began to grow hungry. The sheep and cattle couldn't reach the grass buried beneath the snow. We had not laid aside enough forage in the barns to feed them since no one had known such a winter in the past. The weaker animals began to die, and even the strong ones looked thinner by the day. The old people said they had heard that in their grandparents' day snow had once covered the ground for weeks, but they had always dismissed it as a tall tale. Now we all began to fear those dark days had returned. The last lines of my grandfather's poem seemed to be coming true:

> The cold has seized
> the wings of birds.
> A time of ice has come.

The snow continued to fall in the last few days before Christmas. It was now so deep that it was difficult to walk across the monastery yard except where we had shoveled paths. The food supplies were running so low even before the snow that we had sent home the students who lived near Kildare, promising they could return soon. Bread was served at dinner only once a week along with our thin twice-daily porridge. The sisters and the brothers had all agreed to give their own bread rations to the widows and schoolchildren from distant homes who remained behind.

When I came back into the yard from morning prayers on Christmas Eve, I saw an unexpected sight. Two men were driving a wagon loaded with barrels into the monastery followed by two fat cows tied to the rear. Behind them was a man on horseback. There was so much glare from the sun on the snow that I couldn't tell at first who it was, but then I heard a familiar voice.

"Ho, Deirdre! Beware of Greeks or Leinstermen bearing gifts."

It was Cormac astride a fine black riding mare, large and broad-chested with a silver bridle and multi-colored blanket on its back. The animal must have cost him a fortune.

"Do you like the new mare?" he asked. "She's so beautiful! I bought her from a Spanish merchant. I won't even tell you what I had to pay."

He jumped off his horse in one easy motion and warmly embraced me in front of the church. As I held him tightly, I saw Eithne across the yard staring at us from the widows' hut. I quickly let go of Cormac.

"Cormac," I asked, "is all this for us?"

"Yes indeed," he said. "I don't know if it will feed everyone until spring, but it should help."

Sister Anna and Father Ailbe came out of the church at that moment. Cormac greeted the abbess first.

"Sister Anna," he said bowing from the waist before her, "it's wonderful to see you again. May I present to you and the monastery a few gifts from my kingdom at Glendalough. It's not as much as I would like to give, but three of the barrels are full of grain and the other one has cheese. Both of the cows are pregnant and should give birth in the spring. They are an inadequate payment for all that you and the monastery of Kildare did for me while I was growing up, but I hope you will accept them."

"Thank you, King Cormac. Your generosity is overwhelming in our time of need. We most graciously accept your donations."

Cormac turned to Father Ailbe and bowed again, then embraced him like the prodigal son returned home.

"Father, you're looking well,"

Cormac then lowered his eyes.

"I beg your forgiveness for not coming to visit the last few years. I can only plead that my own father has long been ill and the daily governance of our small kingdom fell upon my poor shoulders."

I could tell Father Ailbe was pleased to see Cormac again. I felt a familiar pang of jealousy. All during our school years I had competed with Cormac to be Father Ailbe's best student. And although he never showed favoritism, I couldn't help but feel that Father Ailbe saw Cormac as the son he never had.

"King Cormac, you bring joy to an old man's heart with your return. I hope you have time to stay a few days so we can talk at length."

"Father Ailbe, Sister Anna, please, you both always called me by my given name and it seems strange to hear any title in front of it from your lips. To you, let me always be just Cormac, whom you taught so well. As for the length of my visit, I'm afraid I must return home early tomorrow morning. My people are struggling with this terrible weather, as is everyone in Ireland, and I must do what I can to help them. But, Father, I do hope we can spend some time together this evening. I brought my text of Homer and a jar of Naxian wine. I even managed to procure some Egyptian dates from a Gaulish sea captain who returned recently from Alexandria. I hope you'll share them with me. But for now, I should supervise the unloading of these supplies."

"You are most gracious," said Sister Anna. "Sister Deirdre, help our benefactor store these goods in the kitchen. Sister Garwen, take the cows to the barn and see that they're fed. And Cormac—"

"Yes, Sister Anna?"

"I expect to see you in the church tonight for evening prayers."

"But of course."

Father Ailbe followed Sister Anna to her hut for what undoubtedly was a discussion about how long the supplies would last. Cormac clapped his hands and directed his men to drive the wagon to the kitchen hut. One of the sisters came forward and took Cormac's horse.

"Was the journey difficult?" I asked as we followed the wagon across the yard.

"It surely was," he said. "The snow is even worse in the mountains than it is here. My horse handled it easily, but the wagon got stuck more than once and I had to help push it out."

"Cormac, thank you so much for bringing us the food. I don't mind telling you, we were getting desperate."

We went into the kitchen and sat down at the table while his men unloaded the barrels, then left us alone together. I brought him a cup of milk.

"I thought you might be needing some food," he said as he drank. "I was hoping to make a good impression on Sister Anna—and on you."

"Well, you have." I leaned across the table and gave him a kiss on the cheek.

"Have you thought any more about my offer?" he asked.

Before I could answer, I heard a woman's voice from the shadows behind us.

"I wonder what offer he made you?"

I turned and saw Eithne standing near the pantry. She must have come through the back door. Cormac sighed and motioned to a chair.

"Eithne, why don't you join us?"

"I don't think so, Cormac."

She walked across the room and stood beside the table with her hands on her hips.

"Well?" she looked at Cormac. "You didn't answer my question. What offer did you make her?"

"Eithne," he said, "this isn't the time. Why don't we talk about it later?"

"Oh, would you like me to come to your quarters tonight? That's the way we did it at Glendalough last summer. We had several long and intimate conversations, if I remember correctly."

I looked at her dumbly, then at Cormac.

"Eithne, really—" he started to speak.

"You mean you didn't tell Deirdre? I'm sure she'd be fascinated to hear all about it. Tell her about how I came to you after I buried my parents and asked if you would consider starting a monastery at Glendalough. I knew Kildare was failing even then. It was only a matter of time even before the fire at Sleaty and the theft of Brigid's bones. I asked if you would make me abbess there. I may be a peasant, but at least I'm a member of your own tribe. When I left you said you would consider it. I was fool enough to believe you cared for me, Cormac, like you did long ago. But you tossed me aside for her then and I see you've done it again. Did you offer to put her in charge of your new monastery instead of me?"

Cormac looked at her, not unkindly, but with firmness that belonged to a born king.

"Not exactly, Eithne. I suggested she might oversee a shrine to Brigid in Glendalough, if the bones turned up. But more important than that, I offered to marry her and make her my queen."

Eithne looked as if Cormac had stabbed her through the heart.

"I think you should leave now, Eithne," he said. "I need to speak with Deirdre alone."

I felt sorry for Eithne as she left the kitchen hut, but I had other matters to deal with.

"Cormac," I said as I rose from the table, "you are the most despicable, duplicitous—"

He stood up and put his hand gently on my shoulder.

"Deirdre, please sit down and listen to me. I think I deserve that."

I sat on the bench with my arms crossed in front of me and listened.

"Yes," he said, "Eithne did come to me last summer and suggest starting a new monastery in my valley. It was an idea I had toyed with before, but when she described the details of Kildare's troubles, I began to think about it more seriously. I knew I couldn't do anything while my father was still alive, so I sent her away with a promise that I would consider it."

"But it seems you enjoyed her company for a while before dismissing her," I said.

"Yes, I confess I did. I'm not proud of leading a nun into temptation, but Eithne was hardly an unwilling participant. And I remind you, Deirdre, that I hadn't seen you then for several years. You had married, left Fergus, and then joined the monastery here. I had no reason to believe you still cared for me. I did not betray your affections by sleeping with Eithne."

I remained facing him with my arms crossed. He had a point. We hadn't spoken then for a long time. I hadn't tried to see him or even contact him since I became a nun. I wasn't happy that he'd been with Eithne, but I couldn't exactly blame him either.

"Alright, Cormac, you had your little fling with Eithne. She's not my favorite person in the world, but it's over and done. It is done, isn't it?"

"Yes, Deirdre. Do you want me to take another oath?"

"No, your word will do this time. What I want to know now is why when we spoke after your inauguration, you misled me into thinking that the idea of having a shrine to Brigid in Glendalough was something you had just come up with? You had stolen the plan from Eithne months before."

"Not really, Deirdre. I admit I didn't give you all the background, but I didn't think it was relevant. Eithne had wanted to start a new monastery independent of Kildare with herself in charge. As I said, I had a similar idea in the back of my mind for years, though not with Eithne ruling over things. I was talking to you about a shrine to Brigid with you overseeing it, though that was only if I had her bones. My offer to marry you wasn't dependent on any of that. Monastery or not, bones or not, I would very much like you to be my wife."

I had unfolded my arms a bit by this point and moved closer to the table.

"But," he said, "this does raise an issue I would like to discuss with you."

"And what would that be?"

"I haven't been able to learn anything about the bones. I did, however, hear about what happened to you on Lorcan's island."

"How did you learn about that?" I asked.

"There are no secrets among thieves, especially when a few gold coins change hands. My contacts told me everything that happened and what Lorcan said to you about the abbot and Dúnlaing's sons. Deirdre, am I mistaken or did I not explicitly warn you not to go to Lorcan's island?"

"Yes, you did. But I was out of options."

"Maybe sometime we can have a little chat sometime about how crazy that was," he said, "though for now I'd like to focus on the future."

"Alright," I said. "Tell me about the future."

"I'm going to guess your next move is to visit the abbot in Armagh and try to threaten, intimidate, or satirize the bones out of him. Am I correct?"

"Yes."

"I wish you well, but let's assume for a moment that doesn't work. The food I brought here will last two or three months at best. My own people are hungry, so I can't afford to give you any more. By early summer at best, Kildare will have to shut down. The students will go home, the brothers and sisters will disperse, and the widows will likely starve to death. Is the picture I paint unfairly bleak?"

I sighed. "No, Cormac, I'm afraid it isn't."

"Then let me propose an alternative, first to you and then, if you approve, to Sister Anna and Father Ailbe—move the monastery of holy Brigid to Glendalough."

Glendalough. The valley of the two lakes. A beautiful place not so far away.

"Cormac, that's a kind offer."

"It's a sincere offer. I know Kildare is a special place chosen by Brigid herself, but Glendalough is an ancient holy site as well. Bring all the monks and nuns. Bring the widows and students. I'll even send men to take apart the church here so we can rebuild it plank by blank at a perfect site I know by the lower lake. I'll grant the monastery the land for the church and the surrounding fields, not as a lease, but as a gift in perpetuity so that it can never be taken away. I will use all my resources as king to support you."

I thought for a minute before I spoke.

"Cormac, that sounds like a perfect solution to our problems, if I can't recover the bones. But let me be blunt—what's in it for you?"

He smiled.

"Ah, Deirdre, do you see why I like you so much? Yes, my offer isn't totally altruistic. I do feel a genuine affection and gratitude to the monastery for all it did for me in my youth, but there's more to it than that. Like I said to you in my feasting hall, I have big plans. Having the monastery of holy Brigid in my kingdom would be very useful to my ambitions, much more so than a simple shrine. It could become the home church for dozens of others in time—first in Leinster, then Munster and Connacht, and finally in Ulster. I dream of seeing the abbot and his Uí Néill kin kneeling before the altar in the church of holy Brigid at Armagh. I plan to be standing there in my royal robes when it happens."

"And I suppose your offer is contingent on having me there beside you as your queen?"

He took my hand.

"I would love that, Deirdre. But, no, my offer does not depend on whether or not you marry me. I will gladly move the church to Glendalough and do everything I said in any case, if Sister Anna and Father Ailbe approve. You can come with them and spend the rest of your life as a nun in the new monastery. Or if you'd prefer, I'll build you a little stone hut high above the lake where you can live out your years in chaste solitude."

I punched him on the arm.

"Very funny, Cormac. But I do appreciate it."

"So, what do you think?" he asked. "Should I talk with Sister Anna and Father Ailbe?"

"I think they would consider the offer. It may be the only way to continue our ministry."

"And should I tell my servants to prepare for a royal wedding?"

It was a fair question. He had given me time to think about it. If I put him off too long, I knew he would have to find someone else. One of the primary duties of a king was to marry and produce sons.

"Cormac, I'm not trying to delay things, but I have a job to finish first. May I give you my answer when I return from Armagh?"

He rose and bowed to me as if I were already a queen. Then he took my hand and helped me up from the table.

"Of course, my dear. But don't tarry too long in Ulster. And please don't underestimate the abbot. He's not a man who will surrender graciously. If you back him into a corner, he will fight."

Chapter Twenty

F ather Ailbe preached a special mass on Christmas
morning before Dari and I left for Armagh. Most
of the snow had melted, so I hoped the journey
wouldn't be too hard. Armagh was far away and most of the
trip would be through the territory of the Uí Néill, the sworn
enemies of Leinster. As a bard I could safely pass through
their lands, as could Dari, as long as she stayed with me.
Still, we were two women travelling alone. We both would
carry daggers on our belts when we left the monastery and
strap knives to our thighs beneath our robes. Within easy
reach in my satchel was a short but very sharp sword which I
knew how to use. I was not the daughter of a famous Leinster
warrior for nothing.

During the sermon, Father Ailbe talked about the problem of
suffering and how a loving God could allow such terrible pain
in our lives. He said there were no easy answers, but perhaps

the problem lay in our perspective. Mortal beings, he said, are trapped in time like insects in amber. But for God, all of time is an eternal present. He said it must be something like the way a parent views a child. A father at his daughter's wedding sees a beautiful, grown woman standing before him, but he sees her just as clearly in his mind's eye as a young child holding his hand as they walk through a field and as a newborn baby in his arms. He said he hoped that someday we would all have that kind of vision so that the trials of this life would make sense at last.

When the homily was finished, Father Ailbe invited all those seeking healing to come forward to the altar. On Christmas the church was normally full of people who were either sick themselves or who had brought loved ones to the tomb of Brigid, but this day there were only a handful present since the bones of Brigid were gone. Father Ailbe reminded us that it is God who provides healing, not the relics themselves.

Two of our elderly widows went forward, helped by some younger nuns. They had been sick for years with pain in their joints and both were almost blind. Father Ailbe laid his hands on their heads and blessed them. An old man named Odrán was next. He was a devout Christian who lived near the monastery and had been at every service I could remember since I was a little girl. He asked Father Ailbe for a blessing not for himself but for his wife who was gravely ill and couldn't make the short journey to the church. Odrán had brought her shawl to the altar, so Father Ailbe placed his hands on the cloth and prayed for her healing.

The last to come forward that day was the family of young Caitlin, the sick girl I had visited with Father Ailbe weeks earlier. Her condition was plainly worse now. She was pale and drawn, with the light almost gone from her beautiful eyes. Her father carried her to the altar in his arms and laid her before the empty chest that had once held Brigid's bones. The rest of the family gathered around him, including Caitlin's mother who held her daughter's hand.

Father Ailbe dipped his finger into the holy water and made the sign of the cross on Caitlin's forehead. She managed a faint smile when she saw him.

"Abba, will the water help me?"

"I hope so, my child, I hope so."

He brushed a stray strand of hair from her cheek and kissed her. Then the family carried Caitlin back among the rest of the small congregation. Father Ailbe concluded the mass with a blessing for all.

I stayed behind to help Father Ailbe put away the candles and other items used in the service. When everyone else had left, he sat down by the empty chest of Brigid, put his head in his hands, and wept. I put my arms around him. He was always composed around others and I felt honored that he would show such emotion with me. He had seen many children die, but there was something about young Caitlin that was wearing deeply at his soul.

"Abba, is there anything I can do to help?"

He shook his head without speaking. At last he composed himself.

"I'm sorry, Deirdre. I don't know what came over me. Maybe I've just seen too many young ones die, children I couldn't help."

"You can't blame yourself, Abba. You can't save everyone."

He managed a faint smile and stood up.

"Please forgive an old man his self-pity, my dear. Now let's get you some breakfast before you start your trip to Armagh. You have a long journey ahead of you."

Dari and I came to the valley of Armagh a week later, having crossed more rivers and streams than I care to remember. Along the way I had told her about Cormac's offer to move the monastery to Glendalough. She was skeptical, just as Sister Anna had been, but neither dismissed the idea outright. Father Ailbe was oddly silent when Cormac talked with him about his plan. When Cormac left the next day, he waved goodbye to all of us from his new mare and promised he would be back for the celebration of holy Brigid's day.

The monastic compound of Armagh looked very much like Kildare except that it was larger and the church at its center was made of stone instead of wood. We found the nuns' quarters at the edge of the complex near the pig pen and sought out one of the sisters, a woman about our age named Macha that Dari had known as a girl. She welcomed us and showed us to the sleeping hut. She was from a farm family near where Dari's parents had lived. The two of them spent some time catching up while I had a fresh cup of buttermilk Macha brought me from the kitchen. She said she would send word to the abbot for us requesting a meeting, but she couldn't promise anything.

Macha took us to the nuns' dining hall for dinner, then to evening prayers at their small chapel. The sisters at Armagh were not allowed to use the church where the monks worshipped. We talked with her that night back in our quarters, hoping to find out something about the bones. I was also curious to learn more about the life of a nun at Armagh. I asked her why the sisters and brothers attended separate services.

"The priests," she laughed, "say it's because we might be a distraction to the weaker monks, though in these outfits I don't see how we could offer many temptations of the flesh."

The nuns of Armagh wore tunics similar to ours at Kildare, but they were bulky and woven from coarse, scratchy wool. The outfits must have been unbearable in summer. The nuns wore Armagh crosses like the monks, but those of the sisters were made from bronze and roughly worked. Instead of leather lanyards like ours, their crosses hung from their necks by small iron links, like miniature slave chains.

"The abbot," Macha continued, "says it's our task to serve God by serving the men of this monastery."

She stood, cleared her throat, and did a hilarious imitation of the abbot giving a homily, complete with gestures.

"My dear sisters, we at Armagh follow the teachings of Christ and the Apostles who say that women have a unique place in the kingdom of God, a glorious, yes glorious calling that no man could possibly fill. Of course, what the scriptures mean by that is that your place is to wash our clothes, cook our meals, and keep your mouths firmly shut."

We all laughed, but I had no doubt there was a lot of truth in her words. Brigid once told me that the first step in oppressing women was to tell them how special they are.

"Not all the monks here are a bad sort," Macha said," but the abbot has everyone under his thumb. No one dares stand up to him."

"Macha," asked Dari, "what kind of work do the nuns do?"

"Oh, they keep us very busy. We're up before sunrise every morning cooking breakfast for the monks. Then cleaning and morning prayers, followed by work in the fields or in the laundry room. In the late afternoon we go back to the kitchen to cook again, then scrub the pots and put away the dishes when the men are finished. After evening prayers we usually sit together in our quarters and weave or mend clothing. Sometimes we make candles."

"But what about teaching the children?" I said. "I saw a school next the church."

She looked at me curiously.

"The brothers teach the boys, Deirdre."

"But what about the girls?"

"Girls? There aren't any girls in the school. But even if there were, we couldn't teach them. None of us can read."

"You can't read?" I was astonished. "But that's one of the first things every sister at Kildare is taught if she doesn't know how already when she enters our monastery."

"That must be wonderful," Macha sighed. "I've always dreamed of learning how to read. It must be magical to be able to know what the words on a parchment say. I've taught myself a few words from old manuscript pages I've hidden away, but the priests would be angry if they knew what I was doing. They say that women shouldn't be educated, that they'll tell us everything we need to know."

I had heard things were different at Armagh, but I had no idea they were this bad.

It was Dari who asked the question that had brought us across Ireland.

"Macha, we're so grateful for the hospitality you've shown us. But I was wondering if I might ask you about something that's been troubling us. Have you heard about the theft of the bones of holy Brigid from our monastery?"

Macha nodded. "The priests told us several weeks ago. You can imagine what they said. They claim God allowed it to punish the sisters of Kildare for their sins."

"Did they?" Dari asked.

"Yes indeed, you sisters are one of their favorite sermon topics. The priests here hold Kildare up as an example of what happens when women reject the order that God has established on earth. They honor Brigid, at least with their words, but they say she was a faithful servant of Patrick who knew her place."

"What?" I shouted.

"Calm down, Deirdre. The sisters here know the truth about Brigid. The priests can't keep us in the dark, no matter how hard they might try. Sometimes at night after the candles are out, we'll gather in our quarters to tell stories about Brigid and pray to her. She means a great deal to us, as do all you sisters at Kildare."

"Macha," Dari said, "why don't you come back with us to Kildare? You could bring as many of the sisters with you as want. I can't promise an easy path ahead, even with the bones, but we'll find a way to carry on our work."

"Oh Dari, that's easier said than done. You were the brave one, leaving and going south to Leinster. The nuns here are little better off than slaves, but this is still our home. You get used to a place after a while, no matter how bad it is."

"But you don't have to stay here. It wasn't easy for me to leave Ulster either, but once I did I found a place where women can make their own way in life—and make a difference. In Kildare we work with, not for, men. We're doing something good there, for the needy, for the children and widows, and for ourselves. It's a new kind of life and you can be a part of it."

"Dari's right, Macha. Come back with us. We can't promise you anything but hard work, but you can start a new life there. I'll teach you to read myself."

Macha looked at me and smiled.

"You know, I just might. I'd love to see the abbot's face when he finds out I'm gone. He'll probably dedicate a whole sermon to Macha, the wayward woman led astray by the evil sisters of Kildare. But who cares? Maybe others would join me in time."

"They would all be welcome," I said. "But we would have a much brighter future if we could find the bones. Macha, I think the abbot stole them."

"Really?" she said, shocked. She considered for a moment, "I wouldn't put it past him."

"I know he tried to get Lorcan to steal them, but that didn't work. He must have found somebody else to do the job. Have you heard anything from the abbot's men that could tie him to the theft of the bones?"

She considered before answering.

"I'm sorry, Deirdre, I don't think so. We're not around the monks that much except when we're serving them meals. I usually clean the abbot's office, but only when he and his clerk are out. None of the other sisters have said anything to me—and that not the sort of thing any of us would keep to ourselves."

"Is there anything unusual in his office?" Dari asked. "Maybe something he's trying to keep out of sight, but still big enough to hold the bones."

"There's a locked chest next to his desk, but it's been there for years."

"What's inside it?"

"I don't know."

I thought maybe I could sneak into his office and pry open the chest that night. But there would be hell to pay if I were caught.

"Macha, can you think of anything that might help us?" I asked. "Anything we could use as evidence against the abbot? If only we had something in writing I could bring before the synod of bishops."

She shook her head. "I wish I could help. I really do. I would love to take the abbot down a few notches, and I don't care if he knows it's me who did it. But they don't usually leave any parchment lying around. I did get some scrap pieces from the clerk's waste bin a few weeks ago, but they just have names and numbers, I think. I've been using them to try to teach myself to read."

"May I see them,?"

"Sure, they're under my bed."

She pulled up the straw-filled mattress and handed me some small pieces of rough calf-skin parchment from underneath.

They weren't the carefully prepared sort scribes make for illus-
trated manuscripts, but leftover pieces quickly done. We used
the same kind at Kildare to practice writing in the schools or for
our account books. These listed the names of what I assumed
were tenants of the monastery and their rents. The final piece
also had landholding records written on it, but the material was
different. The piece itself was poorly prepared, like something
a farmer had cut from a hide and trimmed himself.

"Dari, will you bring me that candle?"

She placed the light on the table next to Macha's bed. I held
the parchment up to the candle. There was something odd
about it. I turned it onto its side.

"It's a palimpsest," I said.

"A what?" asked Macha.

"A piece of parchment that's been used before and had the
ink letters scraped off with a sharp knife so it could be reused.
It saves the time and trouble of making a new writing surface.
Macha, can you bring some more candles?"

When five candles had been lit next to each other, I held the
parchment just a few inches away. I could barely make out the
remains of the old letters crossways to the newer ones on top of
them. What lay underneath were not names and numbers but
some sort of message. The older letters were hard to read, but
fortunately the clerk hadn't been thorough when he scraped
them away. The words were crudely written in the Roman
alphabet with atrocious spelling:

> ABOT—I WENT TO CHIRCH LIK YU TOLD ME—BUT THE
> BONES WER GONE—DONT NOW HU TOOK THEM—WAT
> ABOOT MY MONEY?

"What does it say, Deirdre?" asked Dari.

I threw the parchment on the table.

"That no good, lying, pathetic, son of a—"

"Who, Deirdre? What does it say? Who are you talking about?"

"Look for yourself," I said. "It's from Fergus. I'd recognize his terrible handwriting anywhere.""

Dari held the parchment up to the light and read the words slowly.

"You forgot to add he's a conniving, low-life, stinking piece of—"

"Who are you two talking about?" Macha asked.

"My former husband." I read the words for her. "The abbot must have contacted him to steal the bones when Lorcan refused."

"But Deirdre, when Fergus got there the bones were already gone."

"I know, Dari. The abbot must have realized his mistake in trusting that worm and found another thief who beat him to the bones. But it doesn't matter. Now we have written proof that the abbot hired someone to steal the bones of Brigid. He must have them hidden somewhere in his hut. I'm going to march into his office tomorrow and demand he give them back or I'll haul him before the synod of bishops with this letter as evidence."

"You want me to go with you, Deirdre?" asked Macha. "I'm stronger than I look and I know how to use a knife if he causes trouble."

"I'll come too," said Dari.

"Thank you both, but no. Don't worry about me. The abbot and I are just going to have a friendly little chat. But I'm coming out of that hut with either the bones or the abbot's privates in my hands."

I took the parchment letter from the table and put it safely in my pack.

"And when we get back to Kildare, I'm going to have a talk with Fergus."

Chapter Twenty-One

The next morning one of the sisters brought word that the abbot would see me at noon.

"Are you sure you want to do this?"

"Yes, Dari. It's the only way to get the bones. I'll be fine. But I think you and Macha should take our bags and wait for me by the stream in the woods south of the monastery. I'll meet you there when I'm done. We may need to get out of here quickly."

"Don't worry about me," laughed Macha. "I'm fast as a horse."

I helped them pack, then went to the abbot's hut just as the sun was reaching its mid-point. I knocked and one of the brothers, the same clerk I had seen at Kildare, opened the door. He told me brusquely that I would have to wait, then went back inside and shut the door tightly. He looked like he was afraid I'd give him some disease.

I made myself at home on the bench outside the hut and tried to enjoy the sunny day. The monastery was bustling with the same familiar activity as at Kildare—people scurrying about, the sounds of farm animals, the smells of food cooking—but the striking difference was the look on the faces of the people. At Kildare, we would talk, laugh, argue, even sing as we went about our daily business, but here they all looked miserable. The heads of the monks were bent in prayer or fear, I couldn't tell which. The only woman I could see was a sullen old nun carrying a heavy bag of turnips to the cooking hut. There were also many slaves, all male, who looked like they hadn't had a decent meal in months. They were distinguished by their tattered clothes and shaved heads. A group of them were loading sacks of grain into the storehouse next to monks' quarters.

The monastery had a stable across from the abbot's hut. Sister Macha told me the abbot rode out regularly to survey the monastery holdings and make sure all the tenant farmers were working hard. Those who couldn't pay their rent were thrown off their land. As I waited I saw a monk with a crowd of young boys behind him walk to the stable and stop in front of a standing stone. I assumed it was just a post to tie horses, but as I looked carefully I could see it was a carved figure from the waist up holding his severed left arm in his right hand. The priest was telling the boys this was one of the idols of the foolish Irish heathens who worshipped stones instead of the living God, the creator of heaven and earth. The priest explained to his class that the monastery kept the idol there as an object lesson. When he was done speaking, he urged the boys to throw horse manure at the stone to show their love for the true God.

I was disgusted at the ignorance of this priest and the behavior he was encouraging among his students. At Kildare, we taught our students to respect the old ways even if we disagreed with them. Father Ailbe himself had an ancient, three-faced carved stone he had picked up somewhere on his travels around the island. He used it to teach our students that the idea of the Trinity was not unique to Christianity, but was common among the people of the world for expressing the multiple aspects of divinity. He told us that no one—Greek, Roman, or Irish—ever worshipped a stone, but instead honored the god it represented, much as we honor the cross. When the teacher and students had moved on, I walked over to the stable and used an old rag to wipe away the dung on the figure.

After I had sat on the bench for at least an hour, the same monk as before came out of the hut and motioned for me to enter. He stood as far away from me as possible as he held the door open. I was tempted to give him a big kiss just to see his reaction, but thought the better of it.

The abbot's hut was large and lit with many tallow lamps and candles. There was a wall dividing it in half, behind which I presumed were his bed and personal items. The front section where I found myself had a tall shelf lined with books. There was also a writing desk with a stool, which I presumed belonged to the clerk. Across from it was the locked chest Macha had described, big enough to hold a large treasure—or a small woman's bones. Next to the chest was a massive oak table, behind which sat the abbot. In his lap was a cat, white and fat, that the abbot was slowly stroking.

"Sister Deirdre, it's so good to see you again. Welcome to our humble monastery. I hope your journey from Kildare was pleasant."

"Yes, thank you."

"And I hope the sisters have taken good care of you during your stay. They are such dear ladies."

"They have been most hospitable."

"Excellent, excellent. Please take a seat and make yourself comfortable. Brother, you may go."

The clerk bowed to the abbot and left.

"You must forgive me for making you wait so long. This has been such a busy week for us."

"I'm grateful that you could make the time to see me today, Abbot. I know you have many things to do."

"Of course, of course. I believe it's important for the churches of Ireland to work together. After all, Patrick would have wanted all his children to labor as one in the vineyards of the Lord."

"Yes. I'm sure God himself smiles when the churches of Ireland work together in one spirit."

"Indeed, indeed. Well, Sister Deirdre, I don't want to delay you any longer. How may I help you?"

"Abbot, I'm sure you have heard that we haven't yet been able to find the bones of holy Brigid."

"Yes, I was grieved, deeply grieved, to hear that you haven't been successful."

"I was hoping, Father, that you might have heard something in the last few weeks that could help us. I thought that Armagh, with its great influence and many daughter churches, might by now have had some word."

I studied his face looking for some change or clue, but could see nothing. He never glanced at the chest beneath his shelf.

"You know, Sister Deirdre," said the abbot, "such a theft could never have happened here at Armagh. We maintain a constant vigil of prayer before our altar. There are always at least two members of our community in the church kneeling before the relics of Patrick day and night, not counting the women praying in their own chapel."

He continued to stroke the cat.

"But to answer your question, alas, I must report that I have heard nothing. It is most unusual that I haven't since we have so many friends and supporters, even in Leinster. And it goes without saying that we at Armagh would never be involved in such a nefarious deed."

"Yes, of course, Abbot."

I reached into my cloak and withdrew the golden cross I had found at Sleaty and handed it to the abbot.

"Father, I found this cross when I returned to the ruins of our church at Sleaty. I was wondering if one of your men might have lost it?"

"Sister Deirdre, you found my cross! Oh, I've been wondering where I lost it. Our smith here has never been good at making proper chains. This is the second cross I've lost since becoming abbot. But now, like a lost sheep, it's found its way home."

"I'm glad I could help, Abbot. Do you think you misplaced it when you passed through Sleaty on the way to visit the king at Cashel?"

"No, Sister Deirdre, I still had it then. We passed through Sleaty again briefly on our return trip. I got off my horse to answer nature's call and must have lost it then."

"Was that before the church had burned down?"

"Yes, it was still standing. It looked like it had just been completed."

I wanted to press him about the fire, but I had to remember why I was here. The church was gone. What mattered was the bones.

The abbot continued to look at me with the same placid smile on his face.

I took the letter Cormac had given me and placed it on the abbot's desk. He looked at the seal and opened the letter. His face once again betrayed nothing.

"And what might this be, Sister Deirdre?"

"Abbot, this was found near a ford on the upper Liffey. I was wondering if the seal on the front might be from the church at Armagh?"

He pretended to study it.

"I confess it does resemble ours, but I think it's a poor facsimile. Perhaps one of your pagan priests was inspired, however imperfectly, to imitate the emblem of our Lord in his own seal."

"Perhaps, Abbot. But I'm troubled by the contents in any case. The Ogam writing inside the letter contains the words *Armagh, Michaelmas, Lorcan.*"

The abbot shook his head slowly.

"I can read the words, Sister Deirdre, but I'm afraid someone is playing you for a fool. This is obviously a forgery composed by some misguided soul who wants to implicate the monastery of Armagh in the theft of the bones—as if we would be involved in such a wicked scheme! I would suggest you look instead to your own people in Leinster. It's well known that the sons of King Dúnlaing have long resented their father's donation of tribal lands to your monastery."

"The letter was found on a trail to the house of the king's eldest son."

"Really? Well, there you go. May I ask who found it?"

"Border guards of King Cormac."

"Ah yes, the ambitious new ruler of Glendalough. But doesn't that seem a bit too convenient? A young king seeking to expand his realm discovers a letter that could stir up discord in Dúnlaing's kingdom and turn your king against his sons. That would leave him vulnerable to outside forces. And if Cormac could raise suspicions against Armagh in the lands of the Uí Néill, well, that could be useful to him as well."

"Abbot, King Cormac swore an oath that it was genuine."

"Oh, my dear, I'm sure he did. A thousand oaths! And I'm sure they were convincing, especially to a woman who was once so close to him."

I wasn't surprised the abbot knew about Cormac and me. He collected information he could use against his enemies like a squirrel hoards nuts for winter.

"Be that as it may, Abbot, I heard something else during my investigation that has troubled me."

"Heard from whom, Sister Deirdre?"

"Lorcan, the pirate lord."

For the first time, the abbot began to look nervous. He tried to maintain his calm demeanor, but I saw a nerve twitching on his temple.

"And how did you hear something from him?"

"I travelled to his island, Abbot, and talked with him myself."

The Abbot swallowed hard. I could tell he was both impressed and scared.

"That was either very brave or very foolish, Sister Deirdre."

"Undoubtedly the latter, Abbot, but what I learned was most interesting. He said an agent representing you and the sons of King Dúnlaing had approached him about stealing the bones of holy Brigid. He said he turned down the job."

The abbot pushed the cat off his lap and rose up from behind his desk. For a pasty little man, he managed an impressive display of wounded outrage.

"I must say, Sister Deirdre, I don't care for the direction this conversation has taken. You come to my monastery, receive my hospitality, and then accuse me of conspiring to steal the bones of Brigid. And what is your evidence? A forged Ogam document and the secondhand testimony of a notorious outlaw. You'll never get Lorcan to testify to the synod of bishops. Even if you did, do you think they would believe his word against mine? You have no proof!"

I rose up opposite him. When necessary, I could put on quite a display myself.

"Listen to me, you sniveling little troll. I know you stole the bones. I know you'd like to turn the sisters of Kildare into the same sad creatures as the nuns here, but it will never happen! Do you think you're better than Christ? He came to save women no less than men. He died on the cross for us just as much as you. Women faithfully stood by Christ when even Peter turned his back on him. We were the first to his tomb on the morning of his resurrection and we've been first to serve him ever since. You are a disgrace to God, a disgrace to Patrick, and a disgrace to the mother who bore you!"

The abbot stood with his mouth wide open. I don't think anyone had ever spoken to him like that before, especially not a woman. I kept going while he was off balance.

"I saw the letter Fergus sent you describing how you solicited him to steal the bones. Your clerk tried to scrape away the writing, but I'm afraid he didn't do a very good job. I'm going to take the letter to the bishops and have you removed from your post. You'll be lucky to get a job emptying the latrines here when I'm done with you."

"You—you have that letter? How did you get it? I want to see it," he demanded.

"I don't have it with me, and if I did I wouldn't be foolish enough to give it to you."

He sat down slowly and put his head in his hands.

"Abbot, the one thing that might buy you a modicum of mercy from the bishops is to give me back the bones now. Are they in that chest?"

"I don't have the bones," he cried.

"The time for lies is over, Abbot."

"I don't have the bones!" he shouted. "Yes, Dúnlaing's sons and I tried to hire Lorcan. Yes, I tried to hire that fool Fergus when Lorcan refused me. But somebody else got to them first."

"I don't believe you. I think they're in that chest"

"Look for yourself."

He took an iron key on a chain around his neck and handed it to me. I bent down, turned the lock, and opened the chest.

Gold.

It was full of what must have been hundreds of gold coins, rent from the sweat and blood of all the poor farmers of Armagh. I plunged my hands deep into the chest until I touched the bottom. There was nothing inside but gold.

I had only turned my back on the abbot for a moment when I heard the sound of a sword being pulled from a scabbard. He must have had it hidden under his desk. I jumped up just as the blade came crashing down on the chest where my head had been. I tried to make it to the door, but he cut me off and held the tip of the sword against my throat.

"You little fool," the Abbot sneered. "Did you think I was going to let you walk out of here and ruin me? I may not look like much of a warrior, but I know how to use a sword. I trained with my brothers when I was younger. They laughed at me and thought I'd never amount to anything. They went on to be princes, heroes in battle, but I'm going to outshine them all. I'm going to rule over the churches of this land and bend the kings of Ireland to my will. And you, woman, are not going to stop me. I almost killed you at Sleaty, but you won't get away this time."

"It was you in the church at Sleaty?"

"Of course it was me. I couldn't let you nuns open that church. I knew it would be the first of many if you succeeded. And when I went inside to set the fire, what a joy it was to find a sister of Brigid asleep at the altar. You looked so beautiful there, so vulnerable, almost like an angel—or a devil. I'd burn all of you if I could."

He gripped the hilt of the sword tightly for the thrust.

"Killing me won't help, Abbot. That letter is safely on its way to Kildare. The bishops are going to see it. We'll get the bones back from you even if I'm dead."

"I already told you, Sister Deirdre, I don't have the bones. That was one thing I wasn't lying about. Somebody really did steal them before I could get to them. They've vanished like smoke in the wind. I'll admit, I was greatly surprised, but it works out almost as well for me. If I had the bones, don't you think I would have told the world by now? I would have proudly claimed to have ransomed them from the evil thieves and declared that the good sisters of Kildare were obviously not up to protecting such precious relicts themselves. I'd have no reason to hide them from anyone. I'd display the bones on the altar of our church for all to see."

He pressed the razor-sharp blade against my skin. I felt a trickle of blood run down my neck.

"That letter you found is an inconvenience, but it won't stop me. I'll claim it was a forgery. Some of the bishops have a weakness for gold and can be bought rather cheaply. Without you alive to testify against me, the matter will soon be forgotten. The bones of Brigid may never be found, but neither will yours."

"Abbot," I spoke with some difficulty against the sword, "isn't there something I could do for you to spare my life? Something only a woman could give you?"

I took my hands and slowly began to pull my robes up above my calves, then my thighs. He didn't lower his sword, but he glanced down with a hungry look in his eyes.

In one swift move I pulled out the knife I had strapped to my thigh and rammed my knee into his groin. He collapsed on the ground in agony and I was on top of him in an instant. I kicked the sword aside and held my knife to his throat.

"No—don't kill me—take the gold."

"I don't want your dirty gold, Abbot. Give it back to the starving farmers if you expect any mercy from God someday."

I pulled the linen handkerchief out of his pocket and stuffed it in his mouth while he lay moaning on the ground. Then I bound his mouth tightly with the sash of his robe and tied the rest of him like a trussed pig.

"Abbot, if I were you, I'd lie there quietly for a while until you feel better."

I knelt beside him and flicked my knife gently against his throat, drawing just a drop of blood.

"And Abbot, if you ever mess with the sisters of Brigid again, I will come back and finish this."

With that I left his hut, walked quickly out of the gates of Armagh, and headed off into the woods.

Chapter Twenty-Two

B y the time we reached the Liffey a few days later, I had stopped kicking stones in the path pretending they were the abbot's head.

I had learned a lot at Armagh. I knew now that it was the abbot who burned down the church at Sleaty and not me. I had confirmed that the letter from Cormac was genuine and that the abbot and the king's sons had conspired together to steal the bones of Brigid, just like Lorcan had said. I had also learned, if I hadn't known it before, that Fergus was a greedy, selfish pig.

The one thing I didn't know was where the bones were.

I believed the abbot when he said he didn't have them. People tend to tell you the truth when they're about to kill you—they can't resist the urge to gloat. Besides, I realized he was right when he said he would have put them on display if he had them. It would have made sense for him to use them to attract pilgrims and gain more power.

The feast of holy Brigid was only three weeks away. I had searched everywhere I could think of, talked with everyone I knew, and was now out of ideas and time. As much as I hated the abbot, I had to admit he was right about one thing—the monastery at Kildare would not long survive.

"Dari, who could have stolen the bones? I was so certain it was the abbot."

I had moved beyond worry into despair. Even Dari looked distressed. I knew the future was weighing heavily on her as it was on all the brothers and sisters of Kildare.

"I don't know, Deirdre. But please don't be too hard on yourself, no matter what Sister Anna says to you when we arrive. I don't know what more anyone could have done."

"Dari's right, Deirdre," Macha said. She had been as happy as a spring lamb since we left Ulster. I don't think she had ever tasted real freedom before. "I wish I could have seen the abbot's face when you had him on the floor. I bet you're already a hero to the sisters at Armagh. You've probably made more of a difference there than you realize. They'll never look at him the same way again."

"Oh, I'm a real hero alright, Macha. The only thing I've failed to accomplish is the one thing that matters."

"Deirdre," Dari said, "as bad as things seem, we still have Cormac's offer to move the monastery to Glendalough. It would break my heart to leave Kildare, but at least we could carry on our ministry."

"Yes, it's a generous offer, Dari, but it would change who we are. We're the sisters and brothers of Kildare. We could move the monastery to Persia if we wanted to, but if we go somewhere else, it won't be the same. Besides, I don't know if Father Ailbe would come with us to Glendalough."

We walked in silence for a long time after that. On the path just east of Kildare, we passed by the hut of young Caitlin and I decided to check in on her. I was in no hurry to get back to the monastery. I asked Dari to take Macha and go on ahead and give Sister Anna a report. I would be there shortly to face the wrath of the abbess.

Caitlin had been fading so fast before I left that I wasn't even sure she would still be alive when I arrived, but her mother greeted me at the door and welcomed me to come in and sit with her daughter. The girl was sleeping and looked like a shadow of the lively child I had known only months before. I didn't want to wake her, so I sat by the hearth with her mother to talk.

"Is there anything I can bring you from the monastery for Caitlin? I know Father Ailbe has some stronger medicines to help her rest if the pain returns."

"Thank you, Sister Deirdre, but Father Ailbe was here just yesterday and left some sleeping medicine. He's been so good to us. He comes every few days. On Christmas afternoon he even brought Caitlin a little wooden doll. Isn't it sweet?"

She handed me the doll from the basket near Caitlin's bed. It was the same one that had sat on the shelf in his hut for many years. I couldn't believe he had given this heirloom to Caitlin, no matter how much he cared for her.

"Father Ailbe even came out of his way to visit my little girl back in September on Michaelmas evening, though I knew he was on his way to Munster."

"Michaelmas?" I said. "That's not possible. Your farm is east of Kildare. I walked with him for at least an hour to the west of the monastery to see him off on his journey."

"Well, I'm sure it was Michaelmas. I was at the service that morning in the church. He sat and watched her for an hour or so alone while we rounded up the sheep. I invited him to stay the night but he said he had to be on his way even though it was already dark."

Suddenly I had a very strange feeling.

"I've got to get back to the monastery. I hope Caitlin rests well. I'll try to come back and see her again soon."

I hurried out the door with my heart pounding, not knowing what to think as I walked to Kildare. Why would Father Ailbe go all the way back to Caitlin's hut? Why didn't he tell me?

The monastery yard was quiet but there was smoke coming from Father Ailbe's hut. I knocked on his door.

"Come in, please," he called.

Father Ailbe was sitting by the fire reading. He got to his feet as I came in.

"Deirdre, I'm so glad you made it back safely from Armagh. Would you like some porridge?"

"No, Abba, thank you. I'm still full from breakfast."

"I haven't heard anyone say they were full in months, but tell me how things went with the abbot, as if I can't guess."

"Oh Abba, it's a long story and not a very cheerful one. I'll be glad to tell you everything later. It's such a beautiful day and the snow is all melted. Would you like to go for a walk?"

We went out the gates and down the path to the stream where we sat down on a log.

"Deirdre, my child, what's wrong?"

"Abba, I—I don't know how to ask you something."

"I've found the best way to get an answer," he said, "is to ask a question directly."

"Alright, Abba. Why did you return all the way to Caitlin's hut on Michaelmas after I walked with you so far down the road to the west?"

In spite of the warm sun, the day grew suddenly chilly.

"I had something I wanted to give her," he said at last.

"May I ask what it was?"

He took a deep breath.

"Deirdre, I think you already know."

"Abba—no."

"Yes, my child. I am the one who stole the bones of Brigid."

For a few moments I didn't understand him, as if he had spoken in some foreign tongue. The world seemed to be spinning around me. But his words finally sank in.

"Abba, that's not possible. You of all people can't have taken the bones. You can't be serious."

"I'm quite serious, my child."

"But you're the bishop of Kildare, the guardian of Brigid's holy shrine, the one who taught me everything I know about right and wrong." I was almost shouting at the poor man. "Don't you realize the trouble you've caused? The monastery is on the brink of ruin. People are starving. And do you know what you've put me through? You had me running all over this island looking for those bones. How could you do such a thing? Why would you steal the bones?"

His head was hung in shame. I felt terrible speaking to him like this, but I had to know why he had done it.

"Deirdre," he said, taking a deep breath, "I do understand the anguish I've brought to you and to so many people. You don't know the pain it has caused me. I deeply regret it, but it was necessary—or at least I believed it was. I never meant for any of this to happen. I had hoped that I could put the bones back in the chest when I returned from Munster, before anyone discovered they were missing. I never meant to involve you, I didn't mean to cause you hardship, and I certainly never intended to place you in danger. But, Deirdre, I needed time—time for the bones to work."

"Abba, I cannot possibly imagine what reason you would consider sufficient for stealing the bones of Brigid."

He couldn't even look me in the eye as we sat there together, this man I had known all my life and who meant the world to me. His hands were trembling and his voice shaky as he finally spoke.

"My child, to explain why I did it, I have to tell you about a part of my life I've never shared with anyone. You may still condemn me when you hear the story, but at least you'll know why."

I wrapped my cloak around myself more tightly against the wind and listened.

Chapter Twenty-Three

I 've told you many stories of my childhood in Egypt," Father Ailbe began, "and how I sought out the monastery of holy Anthony in the eastern desert to give myself to God. I was happy there with a life of prayer and study after my wanton youth in Alexandria. We monks needed little from the outside world, but we sold the fruit we cultivated to buy salt and books. The abbot chose me to travel alone to Heliopolis near the Nile every few months with our baskets of dates and olives on the back of an old mule that was even more stubborn than your grandmother. I had friends among the Bedouin tribes along the way and as a child had learned to speak their language from a household slave. Whenever I stopped with them for the night I used my training as a physician to treat their wounds and ailments as best I could.

"In Heliopolis I always sought out the market stall of Amir, a Christian who didn't cheat me as badly as the other merchants.

After the customary bargaining during which he swore his family would starve if he paid the price I asked, we always enjoyed a cup of wine together beneath the palm trees of his home. He had three grown sons and more daughters than I could count, but his eldest girl, Maryam, was the one who served us on each visit. She was as beautiful as Aphrodite, with dark hair and eyes a man would willingly lose himself in forever. As a pious monk, I tried not to look into those eyes, but I found myself drawn to her more and more on each visit. I had been with many women as a young man in Alexandria, but none were like Maryam.

"One evening Amir invited me to spend the night at his home before beginning my journey back to the monastery. I normally stayed with some monks who lived on the edge of the city, but that evening I accepted his offer, hoping I might speak to Maryam alone. Of course, it was a proper home and I never had the chance to see her except in the presence of her family—until late that night when she came to my room. I was so scared I almost fainted, though she was just as frightened. If her father had caught us together, it would have gone very badly for both of us.

"We whispered together of the feelings we had shared in silence for so long. I will spare you the details of what happened next, for you can well imagine. But when I loaded the mule to return to my monastery the next morning, I knew I had committed a terrible sin—all the more for what I had done to Maryam. No longer a virgin, her chances of finding a good husband were ruined. Her honor had been violated, worst of all by a guest, a friend, a supposed man of God.

"I spent the next few months in constant prayer and fasting, pleading with God to forgive me and spare Maryam the shame I had brought upon her. I convinced the abbot to find someone else to go to the outside world in my place. In the sacred rite of confession, I at last told him of my sin. He listened with sympathy, but he knew well the consequences of my actions. I could be forgiven through acts of penance and prayer, but for Maryam there was no refuge.

"One morning I was called from my cell by the abbot to the front gate of the monastery. I assumed one of the Bedouin had come to sell us a goat and the abbot needed a translator, but I was shocked to see Maryam standing there, disheveled and very pregnant. She told of how her father had banished her from her home with curses on both our heads. She had wandered alone across the desert and mountains to find me at the monastery, for she had nowhere else to go. The abbot took Maryam by the hand and ordered food and drink brought to her at the gate, for women were never allowed inside our walls, not even female animals. The three of us sat beneath a olive tree as Maryam ate and drank. There was nothing to discuss. When she had finished, the abbot led out the old mule loaded with what few supplies the monastery could spare. He placed his hands on us both and commended us to God as man and wife. I removed my monk's cloak and handed it to him, then he embraced me like a son and sent us on our way.

"In an isolated valley about two days' journey from the monastery, we came to a spring with grass and cool, clear water. The Bedouin used it on occasion for their herds, but it was too far into the mountains to be a frequent stop on their wanderings. I built a shelter there for Maryam and myself, just a simple hut of stone and branches.

"I was up before dawn every day hunting rabbits and tending to the barley I had planted. Maryam spent her days gathering desert plants for us to eat and turning our little hut into a home. As her time approached, I grew terrified at the prospect of becoming a father, but Maryam talked of nothing but how she looked forward to us being parents. I had destroyed her happy and prosperous life. She could have married a wealthy merchant from Memphis or Thebes and lived in luxury, but there she was with me in the wilderness. When she kissed me at night, I felt so ashamed, but so happy.

"Her labor was long and difficult, but both mother and child were in better shape at the end than I was. She had given birth to a beautiful baby girl we named Ara. I know I was a proud father, but you have never seen such a gorgeous child. She had her mother's eyes and dark hair, with a way about her that made me laugh with joy whenever I held her. I carved a doll for her from tamarisk wood, even though I wasn't very good with a knife. Maryam made a little dress for it that was much better."

"Abba," I interrupted, "is that the doll that was on the shelf in your hut? The one you gave to Caitlin?"

He nodded.

"Yes. I've carried it with me all these years. It's all I had left to remember her by, but I wanted Caitlin to have it."

After a moment, he continued his story.

"As the months passed, I often took Ara with me on walks through our little valley and introduced her to the goats I had traded for with the Bedouin. I told her tales of gods and heroes before bedtime, even though she was too young to understand me. Still, I think she liked the sound of my voice.

"It was the Bedouin boy who was the cause, though it wasn't his fault. Little Ara was just over a year old when his parents came to me seeking help for their young son. He had suddenly become sick the day before with a high fever and swollen glands in the groin and armpits. I had never seen plague before, but I knew the symptoms. I told them sadly there was nothing I could do, but that he might survive if they could keep his fever down. They bathed him in the cool water of the spring that night while Maryam brought them what little wine we had and some rabbit meat, but by morning he was dead. They buried him there with songs of such sadness I wept to hear them. I held my own daughter close and prayed the disease would pass us by.

"Three days after the Bedouin had left, my wife spoke of being chilled even though it was the height of summer. Soon Ara was sick as well. I took them both to the spring and lay them gently in the water, wiping their faces with wet rags. Maryam was the first to die, quietly with a last smile for me in spite of the terrible pain. Ara just lay in my arms silently, looking up as if wondering why her papa couldn't help her. At last she put her little head against my shoulder and closed her eyes.

"I buried my family there beside the Bedouin boy and marked their graves with a wooden cross facing east toward the rising sun. Then I sat down and waited to die. I prayed that the plague would take me away to be with Maryam and Ara in heaven, but it seems that God had other plans for me. My penance has been to live every day since then knowing what I did to Maryam and remembering the eyes of my little girl."

Tears rolled down my face as Father Ailbe finished his story. I thought of my own son and how I had prayed to die after that terrible day. I suppose God has other plans for all of us.

"Abba, I'm so sorry. I never knew. But I still don't understand why you took the bones of Brigid. What happened to your family was terrible, but that was over fifty years ago and far away."

He nodded his head.

"Yes, it was long ago. I tried to run away from the memories, all the way here to Ireland, but of course that isn't possible. Even though I have never forgotten my wife and daughter, I was able to live with the pain until a few months ago when I treated young Caitlin for the first time. Her eyes, Deirdre! She has the same eyes as my Ara. I took one look at her and all the memories came flooding back. I knew I had to save her. To let her die was like losing Ara again. I tried everything, but none of my medicines or prayers worked. I knew the only hope for her were the bones of holy Brigid. I snuck into the church in the early hours of Michaelmas morning while it was empty and took them. I didn't think about the problems it would cause, I just did it. May God forgive me, but nothing mattered to me except saving that precious little girl."

"Did you tie the new ribbon on the latch of the chest?"

"Yes. It was a gift I received years ago as a gift from a king in Munster. I took Brigid's ribbon because it has healing powers as well as her bones. You can add a second theft to my sins.

"I went a roundabout way to Caitlin's hut after I left you on the road and buried the bones beneath her bed while the family was out in the fields. Her parents never knew. I had hoped the bones would work quickly, but when they didn't, I was afraid she would die if I took them away. The bones and ribbon are still there, wrapped safely in oilcloth. I thought having Brigid's bones so close would heal Caitlin, but I was wrong. Now she will soon die just like Ara. I couldn't save either of them, Deirdre. I couldn't save them."

He began to weep. I held him in my arms, not knowing what to say.

"Deirdre," he said at last as he pulled away, "I'm so sorry for everything I put you through, you and everyone else. I'll go now and retrieve the bones. I'll return them to Sister Anna, then I'll resign my office and submit myself to the synod of bishops for punishment."

"Abba, no, you can't."

"I'm afraid there is no other way, my child. I have gravely sinned."

"Abba, wait. What you did may have been wrong, but think about the consequences if anyone finds out what happened."

"I can't hide what I did. A man can only live with so many lies."

"Yes, Abba, you can hide it and you must, for the sake of the monastery and for all of us. If the abbot of Armagh hears about this he'll destroy Kildare. He'll deny he ever tried to steal the bones himself. He'll have the bishops shut down the monastery. The abbot will take the bones to Armagh. Everything we've worked for will come to an end. The brothers and sisters will be scattered, the school will be closed, and the widows will starve to death. Abba, I know you want to do what you think is right, but you have to make one more sacrifice, maybe the hardest one of all. No one must ever know about this—not Dari, not my grandmother, and certainly not Sister Anna. You and I must keep this secret to ourselves, forever."

Father Ailbe sat with his hands folded and his head bowed for a long time. Finally he spoke.

"Deirdre, my child, you're much wiser than I am. I will yield to you in this matter, for the sake of the monastery. I owe you all this much. I will pray to God and blessed Brigid for forgiveness, though I don't deserve it."

"Thank you, Abba. I'll go to Caitlin's house right now and get the bones."

"And what will you tell Sister Anna?" he asked.

"Only that whoever took them did so because of love."

Chapter Twenty-Four

I left Father Ailbe and went back down the road to Caitlin's hut. I knocked on the door and found only her mother inside.

"Sister Deirdre," she said with surprise. "I wasn't expecting to see you again so soon, but welcome."

"Yes, Caitlin was so on my mind as I walked to the monastery that I had to see her again. I wondered if I could have a few minutes alone with her to pray?"

"Of course, Deirdre. I need to feed the chickens anyway. But I don't think she'll know you're here."

After she left, I went to the girl's bedside and sat next to her. I held her hand and spoke gently to her, but there was no response. Her breathing was shallow and her face was as pale as snow. I prayed that God would spare her any more pain, then I knelt on the floor and reached underneath her sleeping platform. I dug away the loose dirt with my hands until I felt the top of a leather bag. I pulled it out and looked inside.

There were the bones of holy Brigid. The linen ribbon was on top of them.

I placed the bundle reverently in my satchel and covered up the hole. Outside I could heard a nightingale singing.

"Forgive me, little one," I said as I kissed Caitlin on the cheek. "I wish the bones could have made you well. No one should have to die so young."

Then I left the farm and headed back to the monastery and the hut of Sister Anna.

"Come in."

I entered and stood before the desk of the abbess. I could see she was busy tallying numbers on her abacus again.

"Sister Deirdre, I've heard the report of Sister Darerca, but I'm afraid I'm too busy to discuss your trip to Armagh at the moment. Unless you've come to tell me there's a wagonload of food outside, I'll have to ask you to leave."

"I'm afraid I don't have any food, Sister Anna, but I do bring good news. I've recovered the bones of holy Brigid."

She looked up at me from her desk, then frowned.

"If this is some sort of joke, I'm not amused."

I opened my satchel and took out the leather bag, laying it gently on her desk. She stared at it for a moment, then slowly untied the drawstring and opened it. She carefully removed the ribbon, then each bone, placing them on her desk. She removed the skull last of all with its unmistakable polished surface and the words SANCTA BRIGIDA carved on the top in Latin. She made the sign of the cross on her chest and prayed silently with her eyes closed. Then she put each bone back in the bag and looked at me.

"Where did you find them?"

"They weren't far away. They were hidden safely the whole time."

"That wasn't what I asked. Where were they and who took them?"

"With the greatest respect, Sister Anna, I'm afraid I can't answer your question. I can only say they were taken with the best of intentions by someone who meant no harm to the monastery."

"That isn't sufficient. I need to know who took them and why."

"It was because of love, Sister Anna."

"Love?"

"Yes. Perhaps it was misguided, but the intentions of the one who took them were pure."

"And you refuse to tell me the identity of this thief?"

"I'm sorry, but I can't. It's for the sake of the monastery and all that we do that I must keep silent."

"And if I insist on pain of expelling you from our order?"

"Then I would leave the monastery."

She looked at me closely before she spoke again.

"Sister Deirdre, you have been a thorn in my side since you put on the veil. You resist authority, you lack discipline, and you seem to think rules are something you need follow only at your convenience. When I put you in charge of finding these bones, I did so only because of your unique status outside these walls. You were willful and difficult then—qualities you still possess in abundance. But as much as I am tempted to remove you from our monastery, I can't ignore the fact that you have accomplished what I asked of you. I'm not yet sure that you were meant to be a nun, but I will tolerate your disobedience on this particular occasion. Nonetheless, let me warn you that my beneficence in this matter isn't to be taken as license. I am grateful you have found the bones and I will allow you to keep your secret, but I expect you to obey me in all things in the future."

"Yes, Sister Anna, of course I will."

"Good. Now go. Tell the sisters and brothers I'll meet with them in the church immediately. We may yet be able to save this monastery."

Chapter Twenty-Five

T he celebration that year on the eve of holy Brigid's day was more joyous than ever before. Word had spread quickly that the bones had been recovered. Everyone from miles around came to celebrate, Christian or not. We had little of our own to offer our visitors, but the pilgrims brought so much themselves it scarcely mattered. We set up tables in the yard and served up more food than any of us had seen in months. There was a bonfire in the center of the monastery yard, with singing and dancing and feasting.

Dari and I walked through the crowd that evening and saw most of the younger brothers and sisters gathered at one table. Macha had just told some story that had everyone in stitches. I was pleased to see how quickly she had fit in. They all greeted us cheerfully as we passed, except for Eithne, who was as hostile as ever.

My grandmother was sitting at another table with a few of the local druids and a couple of the older nuns she had known for years. They were all laughing about something as they drained yet another cup of mead from a barrel Brother Túan had brought. He was sitting near the school, telling a group of children yet again of his life in ages past.

My grandmother waved us over after the others had gotten up to dance.

"Well, my child, you did it." She gave me a big hug. "The question is what will you do now? You know Cormac is here. You're going to have to tell him something."

"That's right," said Dari. "She's got men lined up out the gate wanting to pay her bride price. Now that she's a big hero, it's going to be hard to keep her at our humble monastery."

"Oh, both of you leave me be. I'm going to talk to him now."

"But what will you tell him?" asked Dari and my grandmother at the same time.

"You'll see," I said. "Dari, would you mind bringing Cormac to the church?"

I left them and I walked to the empty sanctuary. The bones of Brigid were safely back in their place now, but Sister Anna had ordered a large iron lock placed on the chest and thick bolts to hold it to the stone floor. I said a quick prayer to Brigid, hoping that I had made the right choice.

Dari brought Cormac in. He looked more dashing than ever in his royal robes and high leather boots. Dari nodded and left. I had a feeling she and my grandmother were listening just outside the door.

"Thank you, Cormac, for coming here." I took his hands as I spoke.

"Deirdre, congratulations about the bones. I heard that you're not revealing who took them. Are you sure you can't even tell me?"

"I'm sorry, Cormac, but I'm taking the secret to my grave."

"Ah well, I can appreciate discretion. I also heard about your encounter with the abbot. Are you alright?"

"Yes, but I think I've made a very dangerous enemy."

"Deirdre, you can't do anything important in this world without making a few."

I took a deep breath before I spoke again.

"Cormac, I've done a lot of thinking about us the last few days."

He smiled and waited.

"But I'm afraid I can't marry you. I'm going to remain here at the monastery of holy Brigid as a nun."

He looked surprised.

"Your offer was so kind, Cormac, and so generous. You would make a fine husband. A woman would be a fool not to marry you."

"But you're not a fool, Deirdre."

"You must understand, Cormac, this is my home now. Here at Kildare is where I can do something good for the world—but I can only do it as a nun. As your queen I would be powerful, but it's not the kind of power that matters to me anymore. There's so much that needs to be done here. We're fighting a war for the soul of Ireland. I realized it when I saw how awful things were at Armagh. If the abbot has his way, the church in Ireland will be a tyranny that destroys hope and grinds down lives of women and men alike. I can't let him win. I've got to do everything I can to fight for Brigid's vision. I don't pretend that there aren't hard times ahead, but this is where I need to be."

For a few moments he didn't say anything. I could hear someone playing the pipes outside.

"Well," Cormac said at last, "I hate to lose you, but I do understand. I don't share your religion, but I don't want men like the abbot running the church either. And please remember that you're not alone. If there is ever anything I can do for the monastery or for you, let me know."

I leaned forward and kissed him on the cheek, then reached up and wrapped my arms around him. We held each other for a long time before I finally let him go.

"It's a pity, Deirdre. You would have made a wonderful queen."

After the last of the pilgrims had finished their dinner and we had begun to clean up, the abbess called me to her hut.

"Come in."

"You wanted to see me, Sister Anna?"

"Yes, have a seat."

I was surprised. The abbess had always made me stand before.

"You might be interested to know I just received some unexpected news. Perhaps the recovery of the bones changed his mind, but King Bran has granted us a chance to rebuild the church at Sleaty."

"Sister Anna, that's wonderful."

"You may not think so once you learn I'm putting you in charge of the project."

"Me? After all my mistakes?"

"Call it an opportunity for redemption. I've come to realize that we all need to put the past behind us."

"Thank you. I won't let you down this time."

"I should hope not."

"But Sister Anna, even with the lands at Sleaty, will the monastery be able to survive?"

"It won't be easy, but with the record offerings of food and animals we gathered today, I think we should be able to continue our ministry until next autumn. Then we'll have to hope and pray that the harvest is good. As for Sleaty, I want to see your plans for building the new church in three days—workers needed, supplies required, estimated completion time—and there will be no excuses if you are late."

"Of course, Sister Anna. I'll have all the information for you on time."

"See that you do. Now go. I have a great deal of work to do."

And with that Sister Anna dismissed me. Perhaps it was just the dim light from the candle in her hut, but I would swear she was smiling as I closed the door.

Chapter Twenty-Six

B efore going to bed that night, I walked back to the church. The remains of the feast had been cleaned up and the tables put away. The guests had all gone back to the sleeping huts or to their nearby homes. The monastery was quiet at last. Tomorrow, at noon on holy Brigid's day, Father Ailbe would offer a special mass for all who had come to Kildare, Christians and druids, nobility and commoners, rich and poor. Everyone would gather together as one to sing praises to heaven and honor the woman who had touched and healed so many lives.

I went into the church and knelt before Brigid's bones. I offered her a prayer of thanksgiving, not just for the recovery of her bones, but for so many blessings—my friends, my family, my community of sisters and brothers—all of us imperfect, all of us still seeking answers.

As I was praying, a young woman pulled at my sleeve. It was Caitlin's sister asking me and Father Ailbe to come to their hut to be with them at the end, for they didn't expect her to last through the night. I quickly went to the nun's quarters to get my harp so that the last sounds she would hear in this life would be sweet music and her mother's soft goodbye. Then I went to Father Ailbe's hut and woke him. I was still angry at him for what he had put me through, for what he had put the whole monastery through, but I knew he hadn't done anything for his own sake. It was all for the love of a child. I held his hand as we walked down the road to Caitlin's farm.

By the time we arrived, her family was gathered around her bedside kneeling in prayer. She was no longer conscious even for short times. Her skin was cold to the touch and her breathing labored and irregular. Father Ailbe was barely able to find a pulse. We all knew her small heart was almost ready to stop. I began to play a peaceful tune, as much for her family as for Caitlin.

We waited there for hours, with her sisters and brothers eventually falling asleep around her. Her father sat on a stool next to her bed. He looked more shocked than saddened, as if he couldn't believe God was taking his little girl away. Her mother remained on the bed beside her, kissing her gently and whispering words of love.

Sometime after midnight Father Ailbe put his ear to her chest to check her breathing. It had became so shallow that I wondered if she was still with us, but then I saw her chest rise slightly and knew she had not yet let go.

The first rays of dawn on holy Brigid's day were piercing the eastern sky when I finally began to drift into sleep. The fire in the hearth had died away with no one tending it. The girl's father was snoring softly by the bed. Only her mother and Father Ailbe kept the vigil.

It was then that I heard a small voice.

"Mama? Why are you crying?"

I opened my eyes and saw Caitlin sitting up in her bed rubbing her eyes as if she had just woken up from a long slumber. She looked tired, but her cheeks were rosy red and her eyes—those beautiful eyes—were bright and shining.

"Mama, I'm hungry."

Her mother gasped and cried out. Her father fell off his stool and the rest of the family jumped up. In an instant they were all gathered around her on the bed shouting and laughing and weeping. Father Ailbe rushed to Caitlin's side and took her hand. Her pulse was strong and her skin was warm once again. The confused little girl just sat there wondering why everyone was hugging her and making such a fuss. At last one of her sisters brought her a bowl of broth that she quickly devoured.

Then, tears running down her face, Caitlin's mother lifted her eyes to heaven with a look of joy I will never again see on this earth and prayed.

"Thank you, thank you, thank you, dear God. Thank you for saving my little girl. It's a miracle! A miracle!"

And of course, it was.

Afterword

J ust a short train ride west of Dublin among the rich
grasslands of eastern Ireland lies the modern town
of Kildare. At its center on a small hill is the restored
Norman cathedral of Saint Brigid, built on the foundation
of a much older church dating back to the fifth century.
Visitors can still imagine the busy life of the nuns who once
lived there. Brigid's bones rested next to the altar of the
church until Viking raids several centuries after her death
destroyed the holy place and scattered her remains—though
some claim the bones were removed before the attack. Her
skull was said to have been rescued and eventually moved
to a church near Lisbon in Portugal, where even today local
people honor her.

Whatever the fate of the mortal remains of Brigid, the legacy
of this remarkable woman remains. Reliable facts about her
life are few, but what we can glean from medieval stories is a

picture of a woman of extraordinary ability and dedication. In a world of men, Brigid stood as a great leader in her own right. How much her legend was influenced by the Irish goddess of the same name is open for debate, though pre-Christian elements are certainly present in the stories about her.

As much as possible, I have used ancient Irish sources and surviving Christian material of the period to create an authentic picture of life in the early sixth century. Pilgrims can still visit the places where Deirdre travelled, such as the beautiful valley of Glendalough, and just south of Kildare, the holy well of Brigid, one of the most peaceful places I know.

If you would like to learn more about the world of Saint Brigid and the next book in the Sister Deirdre series, please visit my website at *philipfreemanbooks.com*.

Acknowledgments

M any thanks to the many friends, students, and colleagues who helped me tell this story. John Paine and his careful editorial eye were invaluable in putting the book together. Joëlle Delbourgo as always has been the best of literary agents. My gratitude as well to Maia Larson and the wonderful people at Pegasus Books. In Dublin, the librarians and curators of the National Library and National Museum of Ireland were indispensible.

About the Author

P hilip Freeman teaches ancient history and languages along with early Irish Christianity and Celtic studies at Luther College in the beautiful hills of Decorah, Iowa. He earned his Ph.D. from Harvard University and is the author of fifteen books, including *Saint Patrick of Ireland*, *The Philosopher and the Druids*, and *The World of Saint Patrick*.